D1495209

old photographs

old photographs

sherie posesorski

Second Story Press

Library and Archives Canada Cataloguing in Publication

Posesorski, Sherie

Old photographs / by Sherie Posesorski.

ISBN 978-1-897187-78-4

I. Title.

PS8581.O758O64 2010   jC813'.54   C2010-904358-8

Editor: D. Rawson
Copyeditor: Kathryn White
Cover and text design: Melissa Kaita
Cover photo: Bart Coenders/iStockphoto

Printed and bound in Canada

*Second Story Press gratefully acknowledges the support of the Ontario
Arts Council and the Canada Council for the Arts for our publishing
program. We acknowledge the financial support of the Government of
Canada through the Book Publishing Industry Development Program.*

ONTARIO ARTS COUNCIL
CONSEIL DES ARTS DE L'ONTARIO

Canada Council   Conseil des Arts
for the Arts   du Canada

Published by
SECOND STORY PRESS
20 Maud Street, Suite 401
Toronto, Ontario, Canada
M5V 2M5
www.secondstorypress.ca

For Irving Posesorski, Jodi Button, and Jordan Fields

chapter one

I was on the late-morning circuit of my daily Tour de France route in Forest Hill. The place name was pseudo, just like everything in it. If there had ever been forests or hills, they were long gone, bulldozed away. The streets barely inclined, and the only remaining green was shrubbery shrouding multimillion-dollar mansions that were as tightly packed together as the row houses on the street where my mom and I had lived in Barrie. The shrubbery – dense, high and prickly – was clearly not there for the sake of garden beauty, but keep-out privacy.

Why the residents even bothered to shield their houses was beyond me. Forest Hill was a ghost town on summer weekdays. The rolling-in-dough residents of these imitation castles, manors, and hacienda-style estates were either at work or on vacation. It wasn't much different the rest of the year, as far as I could tell. The only feet on these sidewalks belonged to public transit riders – the nannies, cooks, and cleaning staff scurrying along to get to work on time. And the only traffic was the service vans summoned to do reno work or repairs. Those and, of course, the owners' luxury sedans – and few of them during the day.

At the start of July, I had zoomed up and down the streets at Lance Armstrong speed (okay, my version of Lance Armstrong speed). It was good for my muscles; my calves were solid by now. However, riding at racing speed left me soaked in sweat, which meant returning midday to my current place of residence, smack-dab in the heart of Forest Hill, to shower and change. I couldn't call it home because it didn't feel like home to me, no matter how many times my mom said it was.

We'd moved there a year and a half ago, after Mom married Dr. Gregory Creighton, the head of cardiology at North Toronto Hospital Center. She'd done a little redecorating, but not much. The doctor, my stepdad – a designation that made both of us squirmy, so I called him Greg, to his relief – often ranted about his first wife, Janice, but he couldn't say she didn't have excellent taste. She did. As huge as it was, the hacienda mansion managed to be comfortable yet classy at the same time. Not an easy feat I'd discovered from my visits to Greg's friends' houses. Most of them looked like museums or high-end furniture stores where you had to be super careful all the time.

Returning midday after a "sweat-o-rama" ride meant facing my mother and her questions about how my day was going, how my friends were doing, and what my plans were. Today, though, I had to return. I'd forgotten my trusty companion – actually my only companion – my BlackBerry Curve.

"You back already, Phoebe?" Mom asked as she opened the door, hoping, I knew, I would stay.

"Only to pick up my BlackBerry," I mumbled, feeling a bit guilty for rushing off and leaving her alone.

She was as lonely in her way as I was in mine – having only my baby sister, Elspeth, for company until Greg came home. Of course, he did call whenever he could to check in. Though he was an extremely busy cardiologist, he still was in the lovesick stage, so that kept the call volume high.

Mom hadn't made any new friends since we'd moved here. That was hard to do, I learned too. I used to feel sorry for her, but not anymore. She had put herself in Arctic isolation by choice. Several of her old friends from Barrie were now living in Toronto too. She had met them for lunch occasionally, but never had invited them to our house to meet Greg and Elspeth. They'd gotten the hint, and the lunches and calls petered out.

Mom could have called her sister and mother in Barrie instead of waiting for them to call her. She could have invited them to stay with us, but she didn't. They hadn't been to Toronto since Christmas, and even then, although Greg's hacienda could have housed a football team, she hadn't asked them to stay with us. During the holidays, they'd stayed at a nearby hotel. They'd gotten the message, as her friends had, and were calling less. Her loneliness was her own fault – so why should I feel one bit of guilt?

"Your friends are waiting for you, huh?" my mom said, sounding wistful but pleased. "Isn't it nice how many new ones you've made."

"Yeah, my friends are waiting."

"What are you planning this afternoon?" she asked.

How I was spending my day with my friends? What friends?

Yuri Kimura was the only good friend I'd made at Dunvegan Academy – the private girls' school my mom had insisted I attend (in one of the too-rare instances when she'd insisted on anything with Greg) to "strengthen my academic credentials for university admittance." And Yuri was with her family in Tokyo for the summer.

Well, I *was* spending quality time with my best friend Yuri, sort of. Only it wasn't in person. It was in text messages and e-mails. Tons of them. Same thing with my cousins and friends in Barrie. Thanks to all that texting, my index fingers were soon going to match my calves, muscle for muscle.

Today's "lie-o-rama" was about to start. At this rate, by the end of the summer my tongue should be as exercised at lying as my legs were at pumping pedals. In spite of all the practice, I remained a lousy liar. My cousin Chris said the key to successful lying was believing the lie as you told it.

Mom was still waiting for an answer. I shrugged, looked down at the marble floor in the vestibule, and then at the wallpaper. "You know, the usual. Biking, a game of tennis, then over to Jennifer's house for a pool party," I mumbled.

"Sounds like fun," she said.

Actually, it sounded like one rotten lie after another to me.

I was pathetic at it. So pathetic it was like I had a neon sign hanging around my neck flashing *liar, liar* in bright red lights. I had all the classic signals of a liar. I never looked my mother in the eye. I mumbled, paused, and garbled my sentences. If my mom weren't so wrapped up in Elspeth, she would have cottoned on already. It seemed like she needed to believe I was living the fantasy life she wanted for me. Therefore, I lied, in part, to save face – mine *and* hers.

Back in Barrie, when I came home from school or from hanging out with my friends, any answer was a good one because my mom and I would share our daily bests and worsts before she went to work her regular evening shift.

Bests like my scoring three goals in a field hockey game. Bests like killing myself laughing at a movie with my cousins, Chris and Adam. Bests like going fishing with Grandy.

Worsts like barreling into the principal like a wrecking ball – and getting a week-long detention. Worsts like getting the lowest grade in the whole class in science.

Bests like Mom being promoted to restaurant manager. Bests like her having saved enough to buy us a new flat screen TV.

Worsts like my mom being screeched at by a super-rude couple because their porterhouse steaks hadn't come fast enough. Worsts like our ancient car stalling in the middle of an intersection and my mom having to wait an hour for a tow truck, only to be charged two hundred bucks for a new battery, when the whole car wasn't worth that much.

After marrying Greg, my mom insisted all our worsts were behind us, and we should only share our bests. However, these days I was feeling as though my bests were never best enough, and not just in Greg's eyes, but in Mom's eyes too.

It seemed like she only wanted me to share the kinds of things that Greg would consider bests – great grades, being popular, being involved in the kinds of extracurricular clubs and activities that his sons had been in when they were my age.

I suppose I could have stayed home longer in the mornings and kept my mom and Elspeth company. After all, it was only when Greg was at work that I could relax with Elspeth. When he was around he had this look on his face like he was going to have a heart attack whenever I held Elspeth, as if somehow I was going to accidentally hurt her. Drop her. Fill her with air like a balloon when I fed her. Give me a break!

I bet I know more about babies than Greg ever did. I'd been babysitting since I was ten. After four years of it, I knew how to feed, burp, diaper, and play with any baby. No complaints – ever – from any of the families I'd babysat for back home.

I'd been trying to get that through to Greg, who behaved as if he was Mr. Familiar with babies and toddlers. In his memories, only! His sons from his first marriage were now in their early thirties, meaning the last time he'd looked after a baby – if he ever had – was decades ago!

There was no nanny rushing up our walkway. Mom was happy to be able to stay home and take care of Elspeth. She'd been working since she was eighteen. She worked all through her pregnancy with me, and went back right afterward. Being at home with Elspeth was her first chance to be a full-time mother.

If I hung around too much in the mornings, I figured Mom would finally realize the "active social life" I was having with my friends was a super-sized lie. She would tell Greg, and I'd be *so* in trouble! He'd imprison me for sure in one of those hideous remedial summer courses he'd been so keen for me to take at Dunvegan. A big baloney story about how all my friends would keep me happily occupied had finally persuaded Greg that I could stay put until late August, when I was going to visit Grandy. So, following some playtime with Elspeth, I'd hit the Forest Hill circuit.

"I have to get my BlackBerry," I repeated, dashing past my mom and upstairs to get it.

When I came down, she was holding Elspeth, who burped, then yawned, closed her eyes, and wiggled as she tried to fall asleep.

My mom kissed her head. "Not too talkative, huh?"

I felt a surge of sympathy for Mom, whose conversation most of the day was one way. "No bests or worsts yet from Elspeth," I said smiling.

"No bests yet…only sound effects," my mom said, smiling back.

ONLY BESTS. How could I forget?

I re-strapped my helmet. "Off on another best-ever day," I said.

My mom flushed, not knowing what had triggered my sarcasm, I guess. She looked at me and I stared back, almost daring her to ask, but she didn't. Instead, she launched into the same spiel that I could recite by heart by now.

"Make sure to wear your helmet all the time you are riding!"

"Yeah, yeah."

"Watch out for cars. Don't go on main streets that have no bike lanes."

"I won't."

"Did you put on sunblock?"

"I did."

"Reapply it every two hours."

"Yes, Mom! I gotta go. My friends are waiting."

"Wait, I have something for you to share with them." She went off to the kitchen and returned with a box of gourmet shortbread-pecan cookies. "Greg says these are the best."

"He would know, wouldn't he?" I muttered, then caught myself. "Thanks!"

If I ate the proof that I had no friends, I'd soon be too lardy to sit on my bike seat. So, the cookies were going where all her treats went this summer – to a food bank donation bin inside the store where I bought my lunch.

"Be home in time for supper."

I saluted. "Yes ma'am. Gotta go!"

"Be careful!" she called after me.

I rode up and down the streets at a leisurely old-lady speed, since it was still stinking hot and humid. I had yet to see a single other person after an hour of riding. Hungry for food and human contact, I headed over to the mammoth supermarket a few blocks away. After locking up my new Schwinn Tornado Cruiser (a much-appreciated present from Greg, who had declared my old bike was too dilapidated to ride safely) I went inside, dropped the cookies in the bin, and walked up the ramp to the take-out section where I bought my lunch most days.

The regular servers, Patty and Steve, weren't behind the counter today. I had been looking forward to stretching out the selection process by yakking with them. However brief, the conversation was always friendly. On slow days, one or the other of them would come over and sit with me for a while.

This afternoon's lunch talk with the server consisted of me

giving my order and the guy behind the counter silently nodding as he passed it to me.

I could have eaten it at a nearby table. However, since I was going to be alone anyhow, I decided I might as well be truly alone, so I packed up my two slices of vegetarian pizza and a pasta salad to eat in my afternoon haunt – the ravine behind the St. Clair West subway station. I rode along the bike path until I found my favorite spot – a leafy, humungous maple tree – and parked myself in its shade. I ate the pizza slowly as I read the latest Agatha Christie mystery, *The Body in the Library*, that Yuri had chosen for our ongoing who-can-solve-the-crime-first contest.

It wasn't much of a contest, or much of a mystery, as to who was going to solve it first, since Yuri was a fanatical reader of mysteries. She was winning without straining her brain cells, unlike me. Yuri had fingered the killers in the other books way before me, and in the last book, way before Miss Marple.

This was the fourth mystery we'd read starring the spinster detective, Miss Jane Marple, whose brain power, sight, and hearing only seemed to get sharper as she aged. She could sniff out clues, find and eliminate suspects, and track down the killer in the biggest crowd of suspects with the single-mindedness of a bloodhound.

Before Yuri had left for the summer, she had come up with this contest. It was her method of getting me to read more. Read period was more like it. I wasn't much of a reader, but the Christie mysteries were easy to read and hard to put down, even for me, the "reluctant reader" as I'd been tagged by my English and history teachers at Dunvegan.

I finished reading and eating, then took out my BlackBerry and texted Yuri my latest, likely feeble, attempt to identify the killer. It blew me away how Yuri could come up with the killer when everyone in the book, except Miss Marple, was a suspect and had a motive for killing the victim.

In this one, I was pretty sure this movie producer, Basil Blake, had to be the perp, given the clues and evidence Christie had presented up to this point. Still, before I got ready to text, I had a second, well, a minute of doubt. Didn't Yuri say that Agatha Christie was the queen of crime because she was the queen of making everyone look guilty? Oh, what the heck if I was wrong...again.

Dear Miss Kimura, the Tokyo Miss Marple, she of the many, never-stop-working-overtime gray cells:

The Toronto Miss Marple, Phoebe Hecht of the less-than-you-for-sure gray cells, thinks it's the sleazy producer, you know, Basil Blake, who did the deed. What do you think? Why isn't Miss Marple in this one much? A few scenes and she's disappeared? What's the deal?

I sat back against the tree trunk, put the BlackBerry down, and took out my iPod. Because of the time difference, I never knew whether Yuri would answer in five minutes or five hours. When my fingers had recovered from typing, I'd text "What's up, Cuz?" messages to Chris, then Adam.

The carbs in the pizza and the heat were making me sleepy. If there was one thing I didn't want, it was to fall asleep under a tree like a homeless person. I stood and did some stretches. As I was gathering up my things to go, I noticed I had a message and sat down again.

Dear Miss Hecht, the Toronto Miss Marple, whose many gray cells are more active than she thinks: (Pun!)

Could be. He's cold and selfish enough to have killed. I'm eyeing the daughter-in-law or son-in-law as the killer. Read on, girl! Miss Marple is nosing around everybody and comparing them to someone she knows in St. Mary Mead.

How's it going? You sitting under the tree now?

A week or so ago, I'd sent Yuri some shots of where I went in the afternoons. She was the only one who knew how I really spent my days. Not that I was embarrassed or anything. I had lots of friends back in Barrie.

It was tough to make friends at Dunvegan Academy. Everyone was real tight. They'd all known each other since kindergarten and didn't exactly welcome new students with open arms. If you were lucky, they merely ignored you. If you were unlucky, you were buzz kill and they made your life hell. I was lucky. They ignored me, and Yuri too. She was new there as well. That's how we hooked up. We'd been in the fall batch of outsiders to be tolerated and generally ignored. Yuri was great. Super smart, but never shoved it in your face or made a big show about it. Funny too, except for her puns.

We'd kid that we were like those pairs of people in newspaper joke photos who looked like twins separated at birth. Both of us had short black-brown hair. Mine was shorter and Yuri had bangs. Both of us had brown eyes and heart-shaped faces. Both of us were skinny, but muscular. Me, from all the sports I did. Yuri, from all those weird exercises that she did: Pilates, tai chi, yoga.

While Yuri was surrounded by family and friends, I was surrounded by bugs, squirrels, and the occasional stray dog. I got pretty lonely sometimes. Okay, more than sometimes.

I was counting down the days like a prisoner in solitary confinement until my visit to Grandy. Till then I had my Tour de Forest Hill and my routine…and all my texting.

I texted Yuri back, then Chris and Adam. I would have told my cousins the truth about my lonesome life, except they didn't need any more ammunition. They already had enough stored up against Mom. Chris and Adam were really ticked off with her because of how she was pushing off Grandy and their mother, my aunt Debbie.

I felt bad for them, especially Grandy, who kept telling us all we needed to be patient and understanding with Mom, reminding us that it would take a while for her to feel like she fit in here.

I was trying hard to follow Grandy's advice, but I prayed Mom would get it together sooner rather than later. Otherwise she might end up hurting them so badly that no amount of understanding would cut their resentment. Just how much longer *was* it going to take Mom to feel confident that was she was good enough to be Greg's wife?

My messages to Chris and Adam were filled with mostly lies about my life. That made them difficult to write because up until recently we'd always shared everything. Adam was my age, fourteen, and Chris seventeen. At this rate of lying – to my mom, to Adam and Chris – I was going to be as big a liar as any prime suspect in a Miss Marple mystery.

All the same, I texted them another tall tale, this one about how some friends and I had taken the ferry to the island to bike, and then I went back to listening to my iPod. I felt myself dozing off again. Fortunately, the rough bark of the tree trunk pricking through my T-shirt kept me upright.

I shook my head and got up. I walked my bike out of the ravine and then hit the streets on my late-afternoon circuit. I took a detour north of Forest Hill, reaching an area of older, small two-storey homes, like the ones I was used to seeing in Barrie.

While some had been renovated, the majority looked like they needed work, and a few appeared as if it had been years since they had been cared for.

I stopped in front of one house, drawn by its garage sale sign. For late afternoon, there was quite a crowd checking out the tables in the garage and lining the driveway.

Now, if there was anything I was an expert in, it was garage sales. Mom and I had sold off everything, and I mean everything, right down to our clothing in the three garage sales we'd held – not that they were held in a garage. We didn't have one; our sales took place on the tiny patch of grass that passed for our front yard.

If there was a crowd here, the stuff must be good. I sighted a bookcase filled with paperbacks and hardcovers. Maybe there were some Agatha Christie mysteries there. If not, at least browsing would kill more time.

chapter two

There were an awful lot of people here. At some of the tables they were as packed in and grabby as customers at a one-day sale in a department store.

I passed by one table displaying a complete set of china and lifted up a plate to read the name of the manufacturer: Royal Albert. Next to it was a table with Mikasa stemware, figurines, and vases. The china figurines were Royal Doulton. Grandy loved those. Last Christmas Chris, Adam, and I had pooled our money to buy her one, a lady wearing a long red dress, holding a parasol. Another table featured Waterford picture frames, knickknacks, needlepoint pictures, and – underneath the table on a blanket – a Singer sewing machine.

A couple of hosers went over to the table with the figurines and started pawing them, hooting and gesturing. Both were wearing tight T-shirts to show off their biceps and abs and had slicked back their longish hair with so much gel it shone like a mirror. One caught me staring and winked, assuming I was attracted to him. *Please!* Then the other one picked up a figurine and tossed it football style.

"Hey!" I yelled. "You break it, you own it!"

I must have yelled louder than I thought because a middle-aged woman called out, "Boys, you should know better!" sounding as if she'd been saying that to them for years.

The "boys," still snickering, strutted away from the table. I watched them for a while, elbowing each other as they looked around. For what, who knew? They didn't exactly look like garage sale buyers. Probably they had nothing else to do.

I headed over to the bookcase. No junk here either. Mostly hardcovers and even the paperbacks, though yellowing, were in mint condition, no broken spines in the bunch. On the bottom shelf, there was one Agatha Christie. In hardcover, too. I pulled it out and leafed through it. The title was *The Murder of Roger Ackroyd.* The detective in it wasn't Jane Marple, but Hercule Poirot. I thought I would get it anyway, since if Christie wrote it, it must be good. Written in tiny, curlicue script was the name of the book's owner, Leah Tomblin, and the price, $3.50. A bargain considering that the paperbacks I'd been buying had cost triple that, and this was a hardcover, as good as new.

Whoever was selling all this stuff off had to be moving. This wasn't your typical getting-rid-of-junk type sale. It seemed to be a contents sale.

Even things I had wanted to keep, my mother had made me put up for sale. Then just engaged to Greg, she was treating everything we owned as stuff you were embarrassed to admit was yours. While some of it was kind of embarrassing – the chipped plates, the faded bed linen, the plastic glassware, the couch with the material ripped on the arms – some wasn't. Was or wasn't, my mom handled everything, and I mean everything, as if it was evidence of the past she wanted to white out, erase, vaporize.

She wasn't sentimental about things the way Grandy, Aunt Debbie, and I were. We hung onto tacky souvenirs, grotty costume jewelry, and clothing that didn't fit anymore because it reminded us of good things and good times.

My mom's vaporization of all of our things at the sale was extreme, even for her – a big mother of a warning sign about how our past was going to be treated from now on.

With Grandy's encouragement, I'd stashed away what I wanted to keep – old birthday, Valentine, and Christmas cards, gifts, school sports awards, old toys, clothes, letters, and costume jewelry. They were stored in a pine chest in the bedroom Grandy kept for me at her house – the bedroom I'd slept in for eleven years before Mom and I had moved to our own house.

Before I went to pay for the book, I thought I'd continue browsing around to see if I came across anything Grandy, Aunt Debbie, Chris, Adam, Yuri, or Elspeth might like. My mom and Greg were automatically off the list since both of them would be insulted to receive a second-hand item.

First things first. I'd better make sure I had the money to pay. I took out my wallet. Seventy dollars. Yikes. I forgot that Mom and Greg were always giving me pocket money; they didn't want me ever to go out without enough, just in case I needed it. It used to be that twenty dollars was a big cash load for me. And that had taken several babysitting sessions to pull together. I'd known better than to hit up Mom or Grandy for cash. Neither of them ever had much to spare.

On a table covered with costume jewelry, I saw some dangling earrings for Chris, an imitation pearl choker for Aunt Debbie, and a rose brooch for Grandy. On another table were old board games. I picked up Trivial Pursuit, one of the early versions, for Adam. A game called Clue looked right up Yuri's alley, and for Elspeth when she got older, an old Snakes & Ladders game. Altogether, my purchases came to forty-eight dollars.

I got in line. There were only five people ahead of me, but it seemed to take forever for the owner, an elderly woman, to calculate the amount of each sale. Twice she had added up the items and the amount owed, only to forget that she'd done it, and she'd had to start all over again. Since most of the people in line acted as if they knew her, they weren't impolite, but I caught several rolling their eyes and sighing.

I would have done the same. What stopped me was the look of confusion and fear on the lady's face, as if she were feeling completely overwhelmed.

As I inched closer, glad to make it to the shade of the garage, I watched, feeling sorry for the lady as she stammered out an apology after short changing one woman. She kept forgetting how much money she'd been handed and how much change she had to return.

Thin and white-haired, with a hardly a wrinkle on her face, she didn't seem to be that much older than Grandy, who was sixty-eight, but what a difference those few years made. Grandy's supervisor at the department store where she worked part-time called her a ball of fire, and that was how she had signed the back of the photo she'd sent me when she'd been chosen employee of the month.

Grandy described herself as being as solid as cement. Sturdy and strong, she was pretty athletic for an older person. She had short, curly, metallic gray hair, blue eyes, and her face was covered with freckles and brown spots from all the time she spent outdoors fishing, boating, gardening, and hiking. It would take a powerful gust of wind to shake her.

Not this lady though. She swayed in her lawn chair, as if the lightest breeze would knock her over, as if there was nothing holding her down. Her clothing was of good quality. She wore a pale yellow shirt and her beige skirt was linen. I knew some about clothing from helping Aunt Debbie with the inventory at the store she managed. Good quality or not, the lady's blouse was buttoned up wrong, and she was missing an earring.

I was almost at the front of the line; there was only a couple in their twenties in front of me. They were trading glances and smirking, obviously assuming the old lady would be an easy mark.

"I'd like to buy that whole set of china," the woman said, pointing to the Royal Albert set I'd passed by. "It's a beauty."

"It is. It was a gift from my late husband on our twenty-fifth wedding anniversary," the lady said softly. "I should have used it often and not just on special occasions."

"Mike and I, we're strapped right now for cash. We recently got engaged and are saving up to get married."

"Massively strapped," he added, his lips twitching, fighting a sneer.

I was sure none of that was true. There wasn't an engagement ring on her left hand. Plus their clothing screamed anything but "strapped for cash." They were both wearing expensive designer jeans, and she had a diamond pendant around her neck – real, I bet.

They just assumed they could cheat the lady because she seemed more and more out of it, customer by customer.

Aunt Debbie had taught me the art of sizing up who was a buyer and who was a browser. A buyer would get possessive with whatever she wanted to buy. Hold on to whatever it was or keep looking at it, as if she couldn't bear to let it out of her sight. A browser was a toucher, not a holder or a starer.

The woman kept turning around to stare at the Royal Albert set as her boyfriend was talking to her. A buyer. That woman wouldn't leave here without it even if she had to pay full price.

And that was what they were going to pay…with my help.

"Mrs. Tomblin," I said, hoping the name in the book I was clutching belonged to this lady, "will only accept the full price. That price is a bargain as it is, and besides, there was a woman here a while ago who didn't have enough cash on her for the set. She went home to get the rest. If you don't buy it ASAP, she will."

While I was lying through my teeth, I was praying that I was convincing and that Mrs. Tomblin wouldn't contradict or expose me. No worries there. She gazed at me as though she believed every word I said. She probably thought she had forgotten the other woman. No time to feel bad about that. I had to nail the sale.

"It goes at the full price. Six hundred and fifty dollars. Take it or leave it."

Good thing I had an excellent memory. I'd seen the price

of the set, written on a piece of cardboard, taped to the front of the table.

"We'll take it," the woman said sulkily. They counted out the cash, and I stuck out my hand. I wouldn't put it past this pair to deliberately shortchange Mrs. Tomblin. I counted it a second time and then handed it to Mrs. Tomblin to put into her metal cash box.

"Thank you, dear," she said. "That was kind of you. I'm not very good at this."

"I am," I said boldly. "Can I help? I used to help out my aunt at the clothing store she manages."

"Hey, you buying or what?" A man standing behind me in line asked.

"Yeah, yeah."

I helped Mrs. Tomblin calculate my purchases, paid her, grabbed another lawn chair, and plunked myself down beside her.

I let Mrs. Tomblin handle the next three customers, but I made sure their purchases were calculated correctly. Customer by customer, she was getting more mixed up and flustered, forgetting the amount, or forgetting to give change, or repeating the amount over and over.

"Can I do this for you?" I whispered.

She nodded, looking mortified and frightened.

"It's the heat; it wears you out," I whispered.

"I guess you're right," she said.

"I'm Phoebe Hecht," I said, then stuck out my hand. "And you're Leah Tomblin." When I saw another frightened look on her face, I added, "Your name was written in the Agatha Christie mystery I bought from you."

"Oh. I thought…maybe I knew you already and had… forgotten…."

"No, no," I said, "We just met."

"I feel like I know you," she added, smiling a little.

"I feel like I know you too," I said. And bizarrely enough, I did. Our getting acquainted session was cut short when several stragglers got in line.

"You rest, I'll manage everything."

"Thank you, dear."

I handled the rest of the sales as Mrs. Tomblin sagged in the chair, her eyes shutting for a moment, and then briefly opening, only to shut again. Why she relied on me, I didn't know. Maybe because she didn't have an alternative and was too tired to protest. Or maybe it was because she thought I looked honest. Likely a little of each.

By dinnertime, most of the people were gone. I looked around and was startled to see that one of the hosers, the Winker, was still here, coming out of the backyard. What was he doing back there? I would have gone and checked, but Mrs. Tomblin was napping, and I didn't want to leave her alone with the money. I stood up and stared at him, hoping he would see me. He did. He winked again. I made a face at him, and he made one back as he swaggered down the driveway.

When he was gone, I counted all the money in the box and wrote the amount on a piece of paper. One thousand, seven hundred and ninety dollars. What a haul!

But at what price? Mrs. Tomblin had sold things she'd loved, things that had been hers and her husband's for decades. And she had to depend on someone she didn't even know for help.

It was kind of depressing to see that she seemed to have no one else but me, a complete stranger to her until two hours ago. It was also kind of scary that she was trusting a stranger (not that I wasn't trustworthy) with her money and things. Thank goodness, Grandy would always have her family to take care of her.

I locked the box and slipped the key into the pocket of the cotton sweater Mrs. Tomblin had draped over the lawn chair. While she continued to nap, I packed up the rest of the things in the boxes and stacked them in the garage, folded up the tables, and with much wheezing, bumping, and probably bruising, I dragged everything else into the garage. How had she done all this earlier? She must have had assistance. That proved she must have friends, neighbors, or family to help her. I hoped so.

She opened her eyes and yawned. I thought she would be astonished that everything was back in the garage, but she wasn't. She just accepted it, very thankfully though, and insisted I stay for supper.

"How much did I make?" she asked groggily, getting up from the lawn chair.

"It was a good sale. One thousand, seven hundred and ninety dollars."

A minute later, she asked, "How much did I make?"

"One thousand, seven hundred and ninety dollars. It's in the metal box. The key is in the pocket of your cardigan."

A minute later, she asked the same question again.

I answered, and then she asked, in a frantic tone, "Where's the key? I lost it!"

"The key is in the pocket of your cardigan," I repeated, trying to sound calm, and not annoyed and freaked out. "You have a key for the garage door? We have to lock it. Otherwise, we'll have to take everything into the house."

"Yes, of course," she said. "I have the key right here."

Right here wasn't right here, and she grew agitated when she couldn't find it in her purse, nor on the table, nor the floor underneath.

"Are you sure you had it with you?"

"I'm sure," she said, sounding not sure at all.

"Perhaps you left it in the house?"

"No, no, it's here."

"Let me look."

She sat back down, literally on the edge of the lawn chair, as I crawled underneath it, looking for the key on the concrete floor, stumbling and almost falling on top of the table as I got up.

"It's not here. It has to be inside the house," I said sharply, and then felt immediately rotten.

"If you say so," she said, back to being passive.

"Let's look there then." I closed the garage door after us. As she unlocked the front door I had this vision that the house would be just like an abandoned mansion in a horror movie with cobwebs and thick dust all over the furniture.

It wasn't. The living room was barren, most of the knick-knacks and pictures on the walls gone, likely among the items that she had been selling, and the rest was packed up in boxes that stood neatly in one corner. On the coffee table, I saw a key.

"Is that the garage door key?"

"I don't remember," she said softly.

"Let me give it a try." I went out and indeed, it was. I locked the garage and went back inside and stood by Mrs. Tomblin.

"Would you mind if I added this to your key chain?"

She nodded and handed me the chain.

"You must stay for supper, I insist. You have been very help-ful," she said, this time sounding like she was going to cry.

It was seven o'clock. Family dinnertime at the Creighton residence. Greg was a real stickler for this pseudo family togeth-erness thing. Like chowing down together every night at seven o'clock somehow made us a family. Made us what he pictured was a family, but he was big on picturing his family. And at the moment, I was ruining that picture.

"I have to call my mother and…Greg to tell them I won't be home for supper." That was true, since it was already dinner-time.

She nodded and stood there, watching. Great, an audience. I fumbled through my knapsack and found my BlackBerry. Shut off. Swell. I had five missed calls. All from my mother.

This was going to be a fun conversation.

"Mom…"

Before I could say more, my mom launched into me. "I called you five times. Your phone was off. I was worried sick. I thought something happened to you. You don't know the city well. I thought maybe you got lost, or…you know what I mean."

I sighed, feeling awful. The city continued to freak her out. She hardly ever ventured out of our neighborhood without Greg or me – only for those rare lunches with former friends. We had never traveled outside of the province. Traveling to Toronto or Ottawa for us had been like traveling to London or Paris was for others.

"I'm really sorry. I didn't turn it off. It shut off by accident in my knapsack. I didn't notice until I took it out now to call you and say I wouldn't be home for dinner."

"What's the point of having a BlackBerry if you don't keep it on?"

I sighed again. She was right. I overheard her whispering something to Greg and him saying something back that I couldn't make out.

"So you remembered to call right at dinnertime? Thank you for that *courtesy*," she said in a clipped voice, now sounding more cross than concerned.

How much of this expressed her own feelings and how much of it was being said for Greg's approval, who could tell?

"I'm sorry. I should have called before to let you know."

"Let us *know*? How about asking our *permission*? This isn't a hotel."

I heard Greg mumble something about me in the background.

I was sorry and guilty about not calling before, but overhearing Greg's disapproving tone of voice doused those feelings fast. I gritted out a clipped "I'm sorry." It was pointless to continue this going-nowhere-good argument. "Yuri's parents invited me to stay for dinner," I lied softly so Mrs. Tomblin wouldn't hear. "Be home by nine." I ended the call before I heard Greg make some complaint about me. I didn't want to hear my mom agreeing with him either.

I didn't need to worry about whether Mrs. Tomblin had listened to me lying. She'd left the living room. I caught sight of her in the kitchen. She was opening and closing cupboard doors as though she couldn't remember where her things were stored.

"Can I help?" This seemed to be my mantra with Mrs. Tomblin.

She stared at the cupboards and then turned to me with an awkward smile. "I can't remember what I was looking for."

"Why don't you sit down...you've had a hard day. I can make us something," I said, feeling a lot less certain than I sounded. I opened the fridge, imagining that if it had any food in it, it would be so rancid and moldy it would be fit only for some laboratory experiment.

My imagining was wrong again, thankfully. The fridge was full; there was fresh milk and cheese, orange and apple juice, cold cuts, vegetables and fruits, and prepared dishes in plastic containers from Max's Marketplace, a gourmet supermarket nearby.

"Have faith in me to put together a potluck dinner?" I asked. "I did that all the time for Grandy."

"Grandy?"

"Oh, that's my nickname for my grandmother. Her name is Mandy and when I was a baby I combined her name with Gran. That's how she ended up as Grandy. My cousins call her that too."

"I don't have grandchildren. My son hasn't married yet."

She had a son! To help her out, to count on – I hoped.

"So, you *have* faith in me, huh!" I teased, feeling that twinge of sadness again that there had been no one else around for her to depend on this afternoon. Maybe her son or some other family member or friend had set up the sale and was too busy to return.

"Of course I do, you're a very nice girl, Phoebe," she said, then sat back and waited for me to pull something together. In fifteen minutes, I had warmed up chicken with rice soup from a can, made a salad, two salmon sandwiches, and a fruit salad.

"That was good, thank you," Mrs. Tomblin declared after devouring everything.

"Do you want me to clean up?"

"Whatever you decide," she said.

Okay, it was ego-lifting to do the deciding. My mother and Greg, especially Greg, did almost all of the deciding about what went on in my life. But it was getting scarier by the minute to have Mrs. Tomblin be so easily trusting, and to have her not want – or be able – to make a decision. What if she trusted the wrong person and went along with some bad decision?

The meal, plus my company, seemed to have revived her. We settled in the living room and immediately she started the story of how she met her husband, Daniel. And boy, was it detailed. So super detailed it was as though she were living in the memory rather than sitting next to me on the couch.

"I was engaged to Ronald Thompson at the time. Daniel was good friends with Ruth and Mike Chudney. Daniel was with them when I met them on the street. It was at the corner of Yonge Street and College, outside where the old Eaton's store once was. It was early fall, cold for that time of the year, and there was a thin layer of ice on the sidewalk. When I turned to say good-bye, I slipped slightly, and Daniel steadied me by grasping my elbow. I felt that…zip…that you feel when you like a man. Afterwards, Daniel turned to Ruth and Mike and announced, 'That's the girl I'm going to marry.' 'But she's already engaged,' Ruth told him. Ruth shared this all with me this later," she said, smiling.

"I was engaged then. A month later, I broke off the engagement, and Ruth called Daniel to tell him and gave him my phone number. He called me right away. On our second date, he asked me to be his girl, and I said yes."

Romantic story and interesting too, but I was struggling to listen. I was wound up thinking about the deep trouble I was in. It was past nine o'clock and I should have been home already. Even if I leapt up from the couch and biked home at crossing-the-finishing-line speed, I was going to be extremely late. I kept trying to leave, but I didn't have the heart to interrupt. Mrs. Tomblin was so cheerful talking about her romance with her husband.

I was also wound up with all the unanswered questions and worries I had about her life. Where was she moving to? How would she manage the move? Who was going to be helping her? Would she lose the money or forget where she'd put it? I was afraid to ask even the most basic question, not wanting to disturb her, now that she was peaceful and happy. My guess was that her present wasn't great, so who could blame her for returning to a past that was. It did throw me that she could recall the ice on the sidewalk from at least fifty years ago, and yet she couldn't remember which plates were in what kitchen cupboards.

The grandfather clock stuck ten o'clock.

"My, my, look at the time. I wasn't boring you with my stories, was I?"

I stood up. "You can tell me more of them when I come back to help you with selling the rest of your things at the garage sale."

She clearly needed assistance. And it wasn't like I was busy and had company during the day, other than squirrels and insects, and on good days, a few words with Patty and Steve.

"You'll come back? That's lovely. Are you certain?"

"Absolutely. I am expert in sales, thanks to Grandy and Aunt Debbie. Okay, not an *expert* expert, but I think I can be useful."

"You are. I would like to pay you," she said, with that frantic expression I'd seen before back on her face and her head turning from side to side.

The metal box with the money must be what she was looking for.

"We decided to put the cash box in the dining room buffet, on the bottom shelf, right here," I said, going over and opening the cabinet door. "And the key to the box is in your purse, in your change purse. Maybe you should write everything down. That's what Grandy does. She makes lists."

When I looked over at her, I noticed all the little pieces of paper lying on the coffee and dining room tables. She *was* making lists. All the same, she wasn't recognizing what they were for.

"I'll be here. I'll remember. When the sale is over, you can deposit the money in the bank."

"Phoebe, I…." she looked grateful and embarrassed. She rose. "Since you are an expert, I should pay you for your work."

"No, no," I protested. I didn't need the money, but she might, wherever she was going.

"Please, I want to give you something. You have been extraordinarily kind and eager to lend a hand. I have several very nice photographs taken by my aunt. Come, I'll show you."

She headed for the stairs and I walked behind her. Hanging on the wall leading to the second floor were six black-and-white photographs.

"My son wanted to sell them. I refused. He said that they

would get a good price. However, I promised not to. He persisted, but I had promised."

She shook, clearly agitated by the memory. I understood just how she was feeling, remembering how my mom had forced to me to sell practically all my stuff at our garage sale. Terrific, two memories neither of us wanted to remember.

"Choose the one you like, and it is yours."

I stood on the stairs. Gosh, they were really good for amateur photos. I could see why her son thought they would sell in a nanosecond at the garage sale. I would have bought one for sure.

I guess people with old 35 mm film cameras took more care composing and taking pictures than those of us with digital cameras did. I merely glanced at the LCD screen and snapped away, not taking the time to set up the picture with the concentration and eye that Mrs. Tomblin's aunt plainly had.

The photographs were all street scenes taken in downtown Toronto (the street signs identified where), and from the clothing the people were wearing and the cars, I was supposing they had been taken in the forties and fifties.

In the first one, two women were standing talking in front of a store on College Street. A man smoking a cigarette was walking past them oblivious to what was going on around him on the street. Beside the curb, two boys were playing with jacks. Two other boys were struggling to carry a huge picture frame, and a toddler on a tricycle paused behind the frame like he was going to fly through, as if it were a portal to a magical place.

I went up a step. In the next picture, two little girls were adjusting the veil on a girl dressed up as a bride, with all the seriousness and attention of adult bridesmaids. Was one of those little girls Mrs. Tomblin? I was about to ask, but decided not to when I saw that she was staring at the pictures as if they were as unfamiliar to her as they were to me.

In the next photo, a bunch of kids were shrieking as they were running through a spraying street hydrant.

"These pictures are awesome!"

Mrs. Tomblin, who had lost interest, was standing on the stairs looking at me, obviously wanting me to hurry and pick one. I was dying to know more about the pictures and when they were taken and her aunt, but I decided, since I was doing the deciding here, that this was not the right time or place.

These pictures made you want to know more. More about the people in them and their relationship to each other. More about what was going on before the shutter clicked and more about what happened after. They were sort of like reading Agatha Christie. There were all these people, and you couldn't help be curious and wonder about them and what was going on between them, as if the picture were a chapter in a mystery story.

"Are you sure you want me to have one? You didn't want to sell them. You wanted to keep them. You said something about a promise."

Mrs. Tomblin gave me a bewildered look, as though she didn't remember what she'd said a few minutes ago. "Please select one. I want to give you one to keep on display."

"I like the one with the kids in the street the best," I said.

"Then that's the one for you. There is some newspaper in the kitchen…no, in the front closet, for you to wrap around it."

As I was doing that, Mrs. Tomblin tapped me on the shoulder. "Can you take these for me?"

She handed me three huge photo albums, the old type where the pictures were held in place with adhesive corners. I flipped through one quickly. In the back were several manila envelopes full of negatives and sheets of tiny photos.

"Your family photos…you want to me take these?"

"Not much room in the little apartment I'm going to at Meadowrest, my son keeps reminding me."

Meadowrest was a retirement home not far from my school. Bad enough the son was making her sell possessions she loved – even wanting her to sell her old family photos – but he also was farming her out to an old age home. I didn't even know him, yet the more his mother said about him, the more I was disliking him.

"You sure you won't have room? You don't want to give these away," I said quietly.

"If you have them, I know they won't be thrown away when I'm gone."

That was such a gloomy thought that I couldn't even come up with something to say for a while. "I'll take the albums for safekeeping, and whenever you want to see them, I'll bring them over. We can go through them and you can tell me about the people in the pictures."

She was too weary and out of it by this time for my attempt to cheer her up to have any effect. I promised to return tomorrow and left.

I had to walk my bike back home, since I was loaded down with the framed picture and the albums. That walk gave me plenty of time to think about how much Mrs. Tomblin's son and my mother had in common when it came to old photographs.

Mom wouldn't let me hang a single picture of Grandy, Aunt
Debbie, Chris, or Adam in my bedroom. I'd hung them up when
we first moved into the Creighton residence. They were taken
down within a month, thanks to the unforgettably gruesome
show-and-tell party Greg had held to introduce us to his family
and friends when we first arrived.

My mom's shame button had been activated big-time by the
"friendly" questioning (think police interrogation of suspects) by
Greg's friends, led by Lenore Simpson, a close friend of Greg's
ex-wife.

Mom and I, Grandy, and Aunt Debbie were on the couch
– sitting ducks for the snobby firing squad. Naturally, since this
was a getting-to-know-us party, we knew we would be ques-
tioned – out of curiosity, out of politeness, and of course, since
all the invitees had been friends with Greg's ex, out of getting
some licks in for Janice.

Lenore led the questioning ("like some Grand Inquisitor
time-traveled from the Spanish Inquisition," Aunt Debbie muttered). She and her friends asked what on the surface sounded
like your typical, pleasant small talk.

"You have all lived in Barrie your whole lives?"

"Yes, and boy has it changed over the years," Grandy said.
"Almost a big city now."

"Really, you think so?" Lenore said. "Traveled much?"

"Ottawa, Winnipeg, Sudbury, Toronto, and St. Catharines,"
we answered.

"Never out of the country?" Lenore asked.

We shook our heads.

"Hmm. What do you do in your spare time?"

"Fishing, bridge, and gardening," said Grandy.

"Birding, hiking, aerobics, and book club," said Aunt Debbie.

"Biking, and all kinds of sports," I said.

"And you Ava, are you into sports as much as your family?"

My mom shook her head. "I don't have much spare time, but I love music and go to concerts when I can."

"A *cultural* interest, hmm."

"What kind of work do you do?" Lenore asked.

"Debbie and I work in retail," Grandy said.

"Oh, really!"

"How interesting, and you Ava, what did you do?"

"I was a restaurant manager at the steakhouse at Casino Rama," my mom said softly.

"Oh! Where did you go to school?"

"Barrie High School," my mom said.

"Oh, really! No higher education?"

"We all went straight into the workforce after high school," Aunt Debbie said brusquely. "Some people don't have the luxury of going to college or university."

Mom then had shot Debbie a pleading look. We knew she was eager to fit in, to be liked by Greg's friends, and we wanted to do what we could to help. We also knew after listening to the dripping-with-sarcasm "oh really, how interesting" chorus from Lenore and her friends that every answer we gave was one more piece of proof that to them we were "Barrie hillbillies," as I'd heard one woman say, not even bothering to whisper.

That party had made my mom go all paranoid about her past.

So when she repeatedly said that it would be for the best to take my family photos down, I eventually did, with resentment admittedly; though I understood how she felt. Now they were in my closet, the albums in my desk drawers, the photos only on display in my computer and cell phone.

And I was stuck having to look at them on the sly as if they were pornography.

chapter three

There was another leg on my Tour de Forest Hill route, but this section I only rode through early in the afternoon when I wasn't drenched in sweat from the heat and from… nerves. It was a small stretch on Spadina Road, a block away from Dunvegan Academy.

The older students from Dunvegan and Lytton Academy, a private boys school nearby, hung out there during lunchtime and after school, at the coffee and pastry shops and Max's Marketplace.

As I rode past the florist and hardware store, and got closer to Max's, I could feel my heart pumping, revving up for a last burst of speed. *Slow down, slow down*, I told my legs. But they were deaf; they pumped away, so I switched gears. *See, if you can pedal like a madwoman in that uphill gear!*

There were seven speeds on my bike; however, on this road I had never yet figured out the right speed. Why? I felt like a stalker on a bike because I *was* a stalker on a bike. My speed depended on how desperate I was to catch a glimpse of Colin Flanagan. He was working as a stock boy at Max's Marketplace.

A glimpse and that was it. Big mouth, fearless me, I had yet to squeak out even a hello as I rode by. The second I glimpsed Colin helping a customer load groceries into a car or hailing a cab for someone, or hosing down the sidewalk, or restocking the fruit and vegetables on display outside the store, I'd gulp for air, and then speed off as though the police were in pursuit.

Colin attended Lytton Academy. The schools allowed the sexes to mingle at highly supervised dances and when Lytton needed a female cheering section at sports and debating events. This was all very unlike my previous school in Barrie where there was lots of mingling – too much for my mother's taste, though there was a twisted explanation for that. She had no worries on that account. I was not like her. Not by a long stretch.

Lytton was famous for its debating club and many of the club members had become prominent lawyers and politicians. It was at a debate last semester that I first saw Colin. To be honest, if I had first seen him at a dance or some other social activity, I wouldn't have noticed him at all.

The debating club needed a bigger audience for its championship rounds, so several classes from grades eight and nine at Dunvegan had been invited over, my class included. Colin was one of six finalists debating in three runoff matches.

He was definitely not the kind of guy you would glom onto right away. He was not a "hottie." He was not a blond, muscular type that would fit in with those guys you see in ads. The ones who looked like they spent way too much time and money on their appearance. Dunvegan was at least a little diverse in its student body, not so rich and white as Lytton was.

The minute he'd started debating, though, every ear and eye was glued to him. In a debate over the benefits and disadvantages of the North American Free Trade Agreement, he'd been assigned to argue against NAFTA.

At fifteen, he looked full grown. He was tall, over six feet and stocky, and it seemed like he wasn't comfortable yet with his body. Ms. Body Language Analyst was deducing this from how awkward he could be at times. And I would know after months of staring at him whenever I got the chance.

He had thick black hair with long bangs and he was always pushing them away from his dark blue eyes. His nose was kind of big and looked as if it had been broken, and his bottom teeth were crooked. It had taken a lot of hovering and staring for me to get those features down pat. When it came to Colin, my observation skills equalled those of Miss Marple.

Colin made a strong case that Canadian manufacturers, farmers, and workers needed the protection they got from tariffs, duties, and protectionist trade laws to keep their industries competitive against foreign ones that didn't pay their workers fair wages, and to keep jobs in Canada for Canadian workers.

Now, free trade wasn't a thrilling topic, and most of the audience had zip interest in it. Yet somehow, Colin made it interesting and important. He'd argued with the smarts of a lawyer and spoken with the smoothness of a politician, a sincere one. Okay, his Irish lilt helped too, as did his sense of humor.

The guy arguing against him, Keith Farrow, came across

as a stuttering shmoe by comparison. Anyone would. It wasn't that Colin was condescending or cutting or sarcastic, it was just that he could counterpunch anything Keith said with firm logic and energy.

Yuri, who had been sitting beside me during the debate, knew right away even before I began blabbing on about him, that I liked Colin. So, in the style of Miss Marple, Yuri's patron saint, she began building a dossier on him for me.

He was brainy; I had figured that out myself. He had been at the top of his class in the two years he'd attended Lytton and had won several academic awards. He was there on a complete scholarship for gifted students. His dad was the superintendent at this rundown ancient apartment building on Avenue Road. (Yuri had found this out by following him and then snooping around.) His family had emigrated from Ireland three years ago, and Colin had two sisters and three brothers.

I had one sort of tortured almost-conversation with him at a school dance in May. He'd been talking with friends, and Yuri had kept pushing me forward until we both joined the group around him. That evening she'd been channelling Harlequin romances and had been whispering romantic advice until she got me next to Colin.

Yuri had waited for a break in the conversation and then had asked him a question about the NAFTA agreement that was in the news – something about soft wood lumber imports. He'd answered her seriously and politely even while his friends were groaning and hooting. Then Sophie, who was a grade ahead of us came over and went all girly and giggly, as she spewed compliments about what an excellent a debater he was. Other than a few nods as Yuri and Colin talked, that had been my conversation with Colin.

A week ago I'd nearly built up the nerve to stop and say hi when I'd seen him come out of the store and hose down the sidewalk. But I hadn't been the only one to see him. A group of his classmates had spotted him too, as they'd exited the coffee shop. They jeered him from across the street, calling him Janitor Boy. (In their books, only certain jobs were acceptable, like working at a coffee shop or a bookstore. Stock boy was too low rent; it actually required work, physical work.) He shrugged them off, even after one especially big idiot had taken his latte and dumped it onto the sidewalk that Colin had just cleaned.

His stiff posture had given away how furious he was, but he went back to hosing down the sidewalk like they weren't worthy of any attention. Not able to get a rise of him, they'd finally left.

If that had been me (and it had been me more than once or twice at school here and back in Barrie), I would have opened my big mouth and matched them insult for insult, fought them too, if I'd had to. This strategy always felt good while I was doing it.

However, I hadn't felt so good when I'd received a month's detention back in Barrie and had been dressed down twice by the headmistress at Dunvegan. And it didn't work either. I learned the hard way that a bullying moron stays a bullying moron, whatever you say or do.

Thwarted by Colin's crappy classmates, I'd raced off until I wore myself out and had to stop to catch my breath in a parkette. I'd never get a chance to really talk with him unless I slowed down and stopped being such a wuss. Why did talking to him scare me? Nothing else scared me. If I kept waiting until the circumstances were perfect and I was in the perfect, self-confident mood, it would never happen.

I pedaled slowly. *If you see him come out of the store, you are going to stop and say hi today or else,* I told myself. *I don't care if you are in a foul mood from last night. It is now or never.*

My mood was the result of the dinner party last night. Greg had invited some doctor associates and their wives, in town for a medical convention, to dinner to meet his new wife and family. My mom had looked gorgeous, like an exotic model, her long hair shiny and wavy, her figure back to being as curvy as it had been before the birth of Elspeth.

She had become as skilled as any diplomat at deflecting any question she didn't want to answer or talking circles around it in euphemisms.

I was not diplomatic, though by now I had been thoroughly drilled by my mother on how not to spill the beans about our former lives. This made me feel like we were living in some witness protection program where the revelation of any information about our past was potentially life-threatening.

The guests asked me polite questions about my family and growing up in Barrie. At each question – even the most everyday ones, like how many relatives did I have in Barrie, what did I like to do for fun, did I like living in Toronto, did I miss Barrie – a flicker of fear would cross my mother's face, as though whatever I answered was going to reveal something she didn't want revealed. Nowadays that was practically every single thing about our past. At first, her lack of trust had hurt, and then it made me fuming mad.

Okay, I got it – boy did it I get it – that everyday questions were still used sometimes against my mom to mortify her. However, if by now even I could tell the difference between ordinary, truly friendly questions and booby-trapped ones, she should be able to as well.

Greg's barely contained terror when I'd been playing with Elspeth after dinner got to me too. She liked to be held up high in my arms. It made her gurgle and smile. Greg had ordered me to put her down immediately as if I had been on the verge of dropping her.

They wouldn't let me leave the living room either. I had to sit there mute and frozen in place until the guests had gone. After all that, being real mature, I'd exploded, shouting, "You two make me sick!" and had run up the stairs and into my bedroom, slamming the door behind me.

I forgot last night as soon as I saw Colin exit the store, carrying several grocery bags. He put them down on the sidewalk and raised his arm to hail a cab. When he had, he went back into the store and came out a minute later with an older female customer. He walked her over to the cab and helped her get in.

Instead of driving off though, the driver was discussing something with Colin and the woman. His voice was getting louder and louder as Colin tried to reason with him, while the woman kept interrupting in a high-pitched voice.

This hardly seemed like the ideal moment to say hi to Colin at long last. I switched gears, preparing to zoom off – yet again – when I noticed that the woman in the cab was Mrs. Tomblin. I propped my bike against a fire hydrant and went over.

"Hey, Mrs. Tomblin, it's me, Phoebe. Is there anything I can do?"

"Finally! Someone to tell me her address," the driver said, sounding completely fed up. He pointed at Mrs. Tomblin. "She can't. If someone doesn't tell me pronto, find yourself another cab!"

I already knew Mrs. Tomblin would completely blank out when she got the least bit stressed. She must have forgotten her address, and from the puzzled look she was giving me, it seemed as though she'd forgotten who I was too.

I went to the car window, put my hand on her shoulder, and said gently, "Remember me? I'm Phoebe Hecht, from the garage sale."

"Phoebe, yes," she said, reaching up to grasp my hand.

"I remember you too, Phoebe Hecht," Colin said, smiling at me.

My heart leapt, it really did, just as poets wrote in love sonnets.

"From the dance. You were with Yuri."

I flushed, happy and amazed that he'd noticed me at all.

"I remember you too, Colin Flanagan, from the debating club finals." (And more, but like I was ever going to let slip how much more, thanks to my stalking and Yuri's spying.)

The taxi driver groaned. "Folks, find yourselves another cabbie. I'm leaving. Talk on your own time, not mine."

"I know where Mrs. Tomblin lives. One seventy-eight Hillsdale Avenue West."

"Hallelujah!" he said sarcastically. "An address."

Mrs. Tomblin was sitting sideways, facing us. "Yes, that's it, that's my address."

"How about I ride home with you, Mrs. Tomblin?" I asked.

"Yes, good…Phoebe."

My bike. I forgot about my bike. "Will my bike fit in the trunk?"

The driver cursed, looking like he would have liked nothing more than to hop into his cab and drive off, leaving us to find another one.

"I'll put it in," Colin said. He followed me over to the hydrant and we lifted the bike up and struggled to shove it into the trunk. This was the closest I had ever been to him. This wasn't actually the romantic first encounter I'd imagined, heaving a bike into a cab trunk together. "Thanks, Colin," I said shyly.

"Thanks for going home with Mrs. Tomblin. She isn't in good shape today, is she?"

Mrs. Tomblin called Colin over to thank him and tip him. We said our good-byes, and as we drove off, I asked her for the address book she carried around with her in her purse. On the first page, I wrote her name, address, and phone number; underneath that, I added my name, my home and BlackBerry numbers, and, in capital letters, Mrs. Tomblin, you can call me any time for help.

I'd ask her later who should be called in case of emergency and write that name and phone number in the front too. Right now, she was starting to calm down, and if she couldn't remember his or her number or name, she would get agitated all over again. I sat back, feeling simultaneously energized from finally actually talking to Colin and blue whenever I glanced at Mrs. Tomblin, wondering what was happening to her. Where were her family and friends when she so obviously needed them?

chapter four

Lying on my bed was the framed photo of kids playing in the street that Mrs. Tomblin had given me. Beside it were a little hammer and several picture hooks. I was trying to decide where to hang it. And I had too much free wall space to choose from. I decided to place it above my desk. I hammered two hooks in and hung up the photo.

Most excellent, I thought. Then, the sight of all the bare walls with no pictures of my family grated, as usual.

There was no picture of Grandy, my mom, or me in Grandy's house.

There was no picture of my mother laughing as she showed Jennie, a waitress, how to carry a tray of food without spilling a drop of coffee, or dislocating her shoulder. There was no picture of Grandy teaching Adam and me how to skate. There was no picture of Chris, Adam, and me dressed up in Halloween costumes. No family pictures of us all gathering together to celebrate birthdays, Christmas and Thanksgiving.

And there was no picture of my mom holding me as a baby. Not on the walls, anyway.

I sat down at my desk, turned on my computer, and started clicking through the images filled with happy memories, which today, instead of making me feel happy, made me sad and lonely and frustrated with my mother.

All those photos used to bring back happy memories for Mom. Weren't they still happy ones for her? They had to be. Yet, it didn't seem like it from how she reacted. How could that have changed? Granted, some of them were ugly-puss pictures that made us cringe, but that Grandy loved. Like the one of me standing slumped in my hockey uniform with my stomach pouched out like a kangaroo, or the one of Adam, his mouth wide open, every chewed morsel of Big Mac on gross display, or the one of Chris frantically trying to get her balance after tripping over Adam's baseball bat.

If only Mom and I could just have it out, once and for all, about the ban on displaying family photos. I preferred the way Grandy and Aunt Debbie were. They said what was on their minds, and that was that. With them I could have made a case for hanging the pictures. With my mother, how could I make a case when we had never discussed it openly? When we argued, I was the one who argued. Mom just traffic-jammed me with euphemisms.

I remembered the time I had let my hair grow really long. It hung like thin, dark string, greasy at the top and ragged at the bottom with split ends – the proof in one of Grandy's most hideous pictures of me. Rather than saying, as Grandy had, "You look cuter with short hair," and showing me pictures that made her point; or as Chris had, telling me that I needed a haircut right now, my mom had danced around it, making remarks like, "Doesn't all that hair get hot on your neck?"

Well, if I couldn't hang up our family pictures without my mother doing her version of freaking out, I'd put up Mrs. Tomblin's. I could tuck them into the corners of the mirror above my dresser.

I shut off the computer and went over to my bed, lay down, and began flipping through one of the albums Mrs. Tomblin had given me – just for safekeeping, I told myself. It was too dismal to think otherwise.

The pictures were a mixture of family snapshots and prints similar to the framed ones taken by Mrs. Tomblin's aunt. It didn't take long for me to figure out the difference between the two. Okay, it helped that the same group of people appeared in the family snapshots: two women in their thirties, Mrs. Tomblin's mother and her aunt, I was guessing, Mrs. Tomblin as a child, a man in his thirties, her father (another guess), and another little girl, who must have been her sister or cousin because they looked alike.

There was an especially nice one of them standing in front of a department store display window decorated for Christmas. Was that the store where Mrs. Tomblin had met her future husband? I took the photo out. And one of a birthday party for Mrs. Tomblin where she was seated at the end of a long table lined with adults and kids, getting ready to blow out the candles on her cake. Skimming through the pictures, I was glad to see that she hadn't always been lonely.

I soon found another method to tell the difference between the photos. Whoever took the family photos made the same mistakes lots of people make. Some of the pictures were blurry, some were taken too close, some too far, some too crooked, some overexposed and some so dark you could hardly make them out.

Mrs. Tomblin's aunt, though, was certainly very good at taking pictures. Hers were kind of like family photos, except they were of various people living downtown. The kids and adults in them were doing the same things you see in family photos: playing games, dressing up in costumes, hanging out, talking together, or walking down the street. Her photos seldom looked posed, though; most appeared as if they had been taken without the people being aware that they were being photographed.

I flipped back to the front of the album, took out several more of Mrs. Tomblin as a little girl and tucked them into my mirror frame.

"You're staring at yourself and you're not ready yet," my mother said, coming into my room with Elspeth in her arms.

I spun around. How much more ready could I get? I was dressed in the outfit she had chosen for me – a black velvet skirt, a ruffled white blouse, pantyhose, black velvet ballet flats, and a fake diamond drop pendant. Not my style at all and even worse, it was as hot as anything outside. And all this winter clothing would only make me feel hotter. We were just going from one air-conditioned place to another, my mother had insisted when she selected them for me to wear.

"A little makeup would help," she said, pointing to my chin. What she really wanted to say was, "You have pimples on your chin and they need to be covered up."

"You *borrowed* my concealer, remember?" I was being sulky, but so what?

I stared at poor Elspeth, whose little face was as made up as an actress at an awards show. My concealer was covering (and not very well) the patchy splotches on her cheeks and chin, and my clear lip gloss coated her lips, though it wouldn't be there for long, given how furiously she was licking her lips. She had on a tight headband that she kept pushing at with her right shoulder, and the frilly floral dress she was wearing looked as uncomfortable as my outfit. She was squirming as though she wanted to make an escape – my wish too.

Only my mother was contentedly prepared for the dreaded family photo shoot. Her long hair, halfway to her waist, was shiny and smooth. Her makeup accented her best features – emerald green eyes and long lashes – and her wraparound jersey dress clung, but tastefully (of key importance to my mom).

I took Elspeth from her. "I know how you feel kiddo," I whispered, trying to stretch out the headband a bit so it wouldn't squeeze her skull quite so tightly.

"What are these?" Mom asked staring at the pictures tucked in the mirror frame.

"What do you think they are?" I muttered. "They're old photos. But you don't have to worry. They're not of us. They are of somebody else's family."

That said, I stomped out of the room with Elspeth.

chapter five

"Greg is *such* a perfectionist," my mother would say fondly, trying to rationalize or apologize for yet another of Greg's rants about someone or something not being up to par. Being *such* a perfectionist at work I could understand. After all, who wanted to be operated on by a cardiac surgeon who wasn't a perfectionist when he was inserting a stent in a blocked artery or doing a quadruple bypass?

The problem was that Greg's perfectionism carried over into everything, things that even my mom had to admit "on occasion" were "unimportant." Greg's eldest son, Matthew, told it like it was – Greg's perfectionism was equally targeted at the stupidest things.

One of Matt's favorite examples was the fridge story. Janice bought a new fridge when the old one had conked out. It was a high-end one, according to Matt; energy-efficient, well-designed inside and out, but more compact than the previous fridge. So there was a small gap between the top of the fridge and the cabinet above it, where there had been none before. Greg had continuously harped about that gap; it bothered him, and he went on and on every time he entered the kitchen about how it ruined the appearance of the whole room. After a month of listening to that, Janice bought a second new fridge and donated the other one to charity.

Greg had the same insanely high standards for human beings. When it came to people who worked under him at the hospital, they were in for a while and then turfed out. At home, cleaning ladies, caterers, gardeners – no one could ever meet his high standards for long. How could they? Even when their work was good – which it was or he wouldn't have hired them in the first place – they were human, and we all fail, make mistakes, screw up at one time or another.

My mother was one of the few people who lived up to Greg's high standards. She worked hard to look perfect, act perfect, keep the house perfect. Sometimes I didn't know how she stood it. It didn't exactly make for a relaxed atmosphere.

Every day was judgment day with Greg. You knew he was judging you and you knew you were probably falling short, which made those who cared about Greg's opinion wary (my mom), anxiously angling for his approval (his youngest son, Jonathan), frazzled (like his secretary), or all of the above.

I wasn't among them because I didn't care. I knew I fell short. I wasn't good at school. I was too interested in sports…for a girl. I was mouthy. I wasn't enough like my mother in behavior or character. I wouldn't ever be good enough to meet Greg's Mount

Everest of expectations, and I didn't care because they weren't *my* expectations.

Matt didn't care either. That was another reason we had bonded so quickly and tightly. Matt gave me a cheat sheet on Greg soon after Mom had married him. We got together once a week for dinner, or a game, or a movie. He really took being an older brother to heart, fortunately for me. He was funny, easy to be around, super friendly – a really good guy.

As far as I could tell, Greg and Matt were fond of each other, but their relationship could get pretty testy. Matt had sided with his mother when his parents divorced. Not only that, Matt was gay, and while Greg tried to be open-minded and accepting, it was obvious that he wished Matt was straight. Matt hadn't gone into medicine like his dad wanted him to. Instead, he worked as an editor at a publishing house.

On the other hand, Jonathan tried like crazy to be a mini version of Greg. His efforts – desperate, sad sometimes – to get Greg's approval made me feel sorry for him, despite how sly and nasty he could be about his dad's remarriage.

I had to admit Greg was right about me in some respects. I knew it would reflect badly on my mother if I didn't try hard to improve in those areas that bugged Greg. Still, he wasn't going to make me a nervous wreck. Not that he didn't make me tense or piss me off. He did. But most of the time I could live with it.

Greg and I had a mutual toleration policy. He tried because he adored my mother, and I tried because I loved her too.

Nowhere was Greg's perfectionism more nutso than in his quest for the perfect studio family portrait, Matt had warned me. How difficult could it be for a experienced professional photographer to take a good family portrait?

When Greg was the customer, it was impossibly difficult.

In the last half hour at Don Hutchinson's studio, he'd told the photographer what backdrop to use, where to place the lights and umbrellas, how to pose us, how many shots to take of each pose, and even how to angle the camera on the tripod.

Of course, the result of all this "directing" was that all the pictures ended up looking the same, whether it was Greg, Janice, Matt, and Jonathan over the years, or Greg, my mother, Elspeth, and me. Forget spontaneity. Every shot was as stiff and unnatural and air brushed as any official portrait of the British Royal Family.

Matt dubbed them "The Creighton Gallery of Stiffs." The portraits of Greg's first family, which used to hang in the living and dining rooms, had been exiled to Greg's den at the back of the house following his marriage to Mom. Now there was lots of room for the new generation of Creighton stiffs.

"Don't you think that strobe could use a filter?" Greg asked, squinting as he pointed at a light to the left.

"Let's break for ten minutes," Don said, ignoring Greg's question. His assistant, Betsy, shut off the hot lights that were making us melt.

"You can all freshen up," Betsy called out. Then catching the disapproving stare from Greg at the implication we needed freshening up, she quickly added, "If you want to. Meanwhile I'll bring some nibbles and drinks."

Elspeth suddenly started wailing like anything, her face getting even redder. I was heading toward the closest air-conditioning vent to dry off when I heard my mother say softly to Greg, "Elspeth's soaked. She needs changing."

"I'll do it, I'll change Elspeth," I said, going back over to them.

"Thank you, Phoebe," Greg said.

It was always killed me that Greg would hardly let me hold Elspeth, but it was fine and dandy for me to change her. Forget him ever doing it! For a doctor who stuck his hands into people's open chests, he was amazingly squeamish about baby crap. He had yet to change her. I swear he'd faint if he had to!

I cleaned, powdered, changed, and fed Elspeth in the dressing room. She fell asleep against me, and I put her down on the chaise lounge and stretched out beside her. I was ready to doze off when Betsy came in, carrying an assortment of soft drinks, juices, and desserts.

"Here, take your pick," Betsy said. "You look like you need reviving."

I sat up and sighed. "Sure do. You too, probably."

Betsy sat down beside me, careful not to wake up Elspeth. "You bet," she said, sighing too, then picked up a bottle of orange juice and slugged it down.

"Are all your clients like us?" I asked, hoping for her sake and Don's that they weren't.

"Some," she said cautiously. "Your dad certainly knows what he wants."

That was a polite way of putting it. And what was a polite way of putting this? "He's not my dad," I said. "He's my stepfather."

I could have said more I suppose, but even with my mom not in the room, I felt censored. Betsy raised her eyebrows, curious to learn more, the rest of her face saying that I should be glad he wasn't my biological father. "Do you see your real dad much?" she asked.

I shrugged. Who knew? I might have passed him in the street every day in Barrie. I wouldn't have recognized him even if I had. He could be any one of three guys, according to my mother. She had been really wild and out of control back then. Only Mom, Grandy, and Aunt Debbie knew the names of those guys. All Mom would tell me was that none of them was good husband or father material.

All Grandy would say to me was that each of them was trouble, and in trouble with the law. Bad news in capital letters. On that point my family had been in complete agreement, so my mom had never asked any of them to take blood tests to find out who was my real poppa.

In this case, ignorance was bliss. In this case, the mystery was best left unsolved, a rock not overturned. So I didn't press to find out who my father was, unsure of whether or not I really wanted to know.

For years, my mother had talked about finding a good husband who would be a good father for me. It wasn't like there was a shortage of men who wanted to date her. But by the time she'd been promoted to manager of the steakhouse three years ago, she wasn't about to get hooked up with a guy who wasn't as driven and ambitious as she was. While some of the men she'd dated had been good father material, at least in my opinion, they weren't good husband material in hers.

Obviously, she thought Greg was both. And I guess in most ways he was. In some ways, though, he just wasn't.

Evidently, Betsy could see that. "What a control freak! He makes it hard for you to see your dad, doesn't he?"

I was saved from having to come up with some lying answer to that when Don rushed in. "Dr. and Mrs. Creighton are thirsty, remember?" he said brusquely.

"I remember," Betsy said, rolling her eyes. Greg must have demanded refreshments, and as he did with waiters at restaurants, he wanted service in a fingersnap. Faster.

"My fault," I said, jumping in. "Betsy was helping me change Elspeth."

Betsy squeezed my arm in gratitude (boy, at this rate, I was going to be a professional liar with all the practice I was getting) as she got up and left with the tray.

"Time to go back?" I asked Don.

He nodded.

I hated to wake Elspeth but I tickled her on her stomach until she was giggling, and then brought her back out into the studio.

By this point Don had given up control to Greg.

"Can we have a shot here of Ava, just with Elspeth?" Greg said, getting up off the couch and standing off to the side. I stood and moved off to the other side.

After a number of shots were taken, Greg began edging closer to the couch. I got it. It shouldn't have bothered me, but it did. He was getting into position for the money shot – the three of them without me.

"I'm going to stand here, behind them," Greg said.

I saw my mom open her mouth to ask where I should be positioned.

"I'm baking in here. I'm going outside," I said, not wanting to be forced into the picture by her intervention.

"Don't you want to be in this picture too?" she asked, looking troubled. That look quickly changed to panic as Greg began tapping his foot and sighing dramatically. She needed to get on board with what he wanted.

"I'm sure. I've had it for now," I said, going over to kiss her and Elspeth. Glimpsing the smug expression on Greg's face, I rushed toward the exit.

I paced in the back alleyway. I knew what Greg was like, so it was pointless in the extreme to get upset, but I was all the same. In moments like this it sure seemed like Greg's vision of his new picture-perfect family didn't include me.

chapter six

Here we were, almost all gathered together in Greg's favorite midtown bistro, one big, fill-in-the-blank family. How you filled in the blank depended on which one of us you were.

Now Greg, who was oblivious to the feelings of others unless they spelled it out for him by crying, laughing, or screaming, saw us as one big happy family because none of us was crying or screaming – yet.

My mom politely ignored what she had to. That came from years of practice as an unwed mother and from working in the food industry where the customer was always right, no matter how rude, demanding, or condescending.

She was aware of Jonathan's disgust with her, and with Greg for marrying her. Nevertheless, she gazed at him as if she liked him and he liked her. I admired her for being able to do that. I would have matched his death-ray stares with killer glares of my own.

Jonathan, whose dislike of my mom was growing at super-sonic speed, presumed that he hid it well under his smarmy pretence of being friendly. His girlfriend, Michelle, was just as smarmy. Greg was the only one who didn't get the fact that Jonathan considered my mom a trophy wife, and not much of a trophy at that.

Jonathan had gone into medicine, as Greg had desired. Not dexterous enough to be a surgeon, he was in the last year of his residency, studying neurology. His girlfriend had recently joined a dermatology practice.

I had tuned out the conversation twenty minutes back, putting myself on medical leave. I had already heard more than I wanted to hear for the rest of my life about heart valve replacement surgery from Greg, the latest in the treatment of Parkinson's disease from Jonathan, and injectable fillers from Michelle. From the look of Michelle's fish lips, it seemed to me she must be dipping into the collagen between patients.

I wished Elspeth was here to play with, but she was at home with a sitter, and Matt, my savior, had called to say he was stuck in traffic and would be late. Even with Matt sitting beside me, whispering funny comments into my ear, these twice-monthly meals were boring to the extreme. And they felt endless, no matter how short or long our unhappy meal was.

Back in Barrie, dinners out with our whole family had been as entertaining as watching some sitcom. Everybody gave you the skinny on everything going on in his or her life, even when you wished sometimes they wouldn't go into *that* much detail.

I was thrilled that, at long last, another installment of those family dinners would take place in two weeks, when Grandy and Aunt Debbie were coming to Toronto for a retail convention and bringing Adam along.

"In la-la land already, kiddo?" Matt teased softly, kissing me on the head, as he slipped into the chair beside me. "My apologies," he said to the rest of the table. "Traffic on Avenue Road was a bitch, all that construction."

"They let you wear *that* to work?" Greg said as greeting to Matt.

"You think I'm overdressed?" Matt fired back. "I was worried about that this morning, too."

I had to bite my lip not to laugh. Matt was wearing a peacock-blue, orange, and yellow Hawaiian shirt, olive cargo pants, and black flip-flops. From studying the exiled portraits in Greg's den, it seemed to me that Matt was a mix of Greg and his mother. Like Janice, he had thick, dirty-blond hair and a long, horse-shaped face. He'd often groan to me about his appearance. Why couldn't he have inherited his mother's ocean blue eyes and noble nose instead, he'd moan.

Actually, he looked like Greg, too, a lot more than Jonathan did, which probably annoyed Jonathan. It appeared that most everything about Matt annoyed Jonathan. Matt had the lean, wiry build of a runner, and stayed lean, no matter how much he ate. And he did eat, as he would always joke, like a horse.

Jonathan was shorter, and was working meal by meal toward being stout. Though he had inherited Greg's dark hair color, unlike Greg who still had a full head of hair (suspiciously dark for a middle-aged guy), Jonathan had also inherited some male relative's going-bald-really-early gene. He already had a bald spot at the top of his head. He sweated to mimic Greg by dressing like him – nothing funky or stylish for Jonathan, ever. Casual meant polo shirts, Bermuda shorts, and topsiders in the summer; corduroy pants, striped shirts, pullover sweaters, and loafers in the winter.

Tonight, Greg and Jonathan both, naturally, were dressed in expensive suits, as was Michelle who was wearing a black pantsuit. My mother's sleeveless lavender dress highlighted her latest gifts from Greg – a large circular diamond pendant, matching diamond loop earrings, and a diamond tennis bracelet. Jonathan had no doubt already calculated how much the cost of those had cut into his inheritance.

Since I regularly visited Matt at work, I knew he usually wore some bland-colored shirt, khakis, socks, and brogues to work. Dressing like this and shoving being gay in Greg's face was his way of flipping his finger at his father. And who could blame him?

I reached over and grabbed his hand. "I'm glad you're here."

He squeezed back. "Double dose back, kiddo."

"Hey, I've got some dish to share," he said conspiratorially as he bent forward. "Paul Norman thinks the flimsy, illiterate and incoherent piece of drivel that he is faxing in, chapter by chapter, will fulfill the terms of his contract. Think again, Paulie! We want every single word of the hundred-thousand word mystery thriller you promised, or we are going to sue you right out of your ritzy condo into public housing."

"It's a mystery how he ever wrote a mystery," I added, repeating what Matt always said at the conclusion of another story about just how demented Paul Norman was. Matt smiled and then told the others the story he'd told me last week about how the best-selling author had been dumped on him.

Norman, the cheapest of cheapskates, always brought his lunch in a brown paper bag during editing sessions. Matt said he was all for recycling, but Norman used the same brown paper bag over and over, until it got so worn and torn that you could follow the trail of crumbs he left in the office. Two weeks ago, Norman had gone to a nearby park to eat his lunch.

Afterwards, he had brought back in the paper bag a small garter snake he'd befriended. "Like meets like," as Matt quipped. He placed the bag on the previous editor's desk next to the manuscript. The snake eventually slithered out of the bag and across the desk. His editor shrieked and continued to shriek until they found someone in the office willing to grab the snake, put it back in the bag, and return it to the park. That editor had refused to work on Norman's books anymore. Matt had all of us laughing. He said he was going to demand combat pay for taking on the nutcase.

As expected, being competitive and jealous of Matt, Jonathan then felt compelled to top that story. Good luck. Jonathan couldn't tell an exciting story, if he'd ever had one to tell, which I seriously doubted. The story he was telling now about all the prominent celebrities he had seen at the hospital's fundraiser was like listening to a teacher reciting a class attendance list.

"How goes the latest Madame Tussauds' waxwork photo session?" Matt whispered, evidently as bored as I was with Jonathan's namedropping.

I giggled; I couldn't help it because that was exactly what Greg achieved – family photos as formal and official and dead-looking as one of the museum's wax reproductions of famous people.

"Oh, you know," I whispered, shrugging.

"Yes, I know, I really know," Matt said dramatically.

"You know what?" Jonathan said, glaring at Matt.

"I realize, Bro, that your storytelling skills are limited, but really, do you need to recite the name of every bigwig at the fundraiser? Just e-mail us the guest list, *please*!"

I had to bite my lips again to contain a major case of giggles. From the corner of my eye, I saw my mother swallowing her laughter with several sips of wine.

Then I caught Jonathan nodding his head, as though he were giving Michelle a go-ahead signal.

"Jon, have you told your father and Ava about how we met?" Michelle asked, smiling a big phoney smile. I did admire her super-white teeth, though their whiteness was as fake as that smile.

"My dear, what a blinding smile you have," Matt said. "I need sunglasses." I tapped Matt's ankle, and he tapped me right back. Maybe this dinner wouldn't be so boring after all.

Michelle deliberately turned her head toward Greg and my mom. "Jon and I met at a dinner party. Our mutual friends had set us up…but not with each other. But, the minute we saw each other, we were just drawn together—"

"Like paper clips to the bottom of a magnetized stapler," Matt threw in. "How romantic!"

Michelle frowned at Matt. "It was."

"Can you let her continue, please?" Jonathan said.

Matt put his fingers behind his ears and flipped them forward. "I'm all ears."

Glaring at Matt, Michelle went on. "It was love at first sight, and we've been together ever since."

"How long has it been? Three weeks? What a love story. Cue the violins!" Matt said, gesturing like he was playing one.

"Was your meeting with Greg just as romantic, Ava?" Michelle asked in this bogus sweet voice.

This was a setup! Jonathan had enlisted Michelle to dig up dirt on my mother. Ever since Greg and my mom had married, he'd been trying to wheedle more than just generalities out of her about her past. Good luck, Mister!

Even Jonathan, whose lack of people-reading skills beat those of Greg, had clued in to the fact that my mother wanted to avoid any conversations about her past. Her answers were smooth but vague, and as soon as she could politely manage it, she changed the subject.

"We met at the steakhouse at Casino Rama in Barrie," Mom said, a telltale flush staining her cheeks.

"You were both there gambling?" Michelle asked.

"No, I was there gambling," Greg cut in, taking hold of my mother's hand. "I was attending a medical convention in Barrie, and they scheduled an evening of gambling there for us to let off steam. Ava was the restaurant's manager, and she greeted our group since we'd reserved the whole place for the evening."

"Later on I was doing a run-through of the restaurant to make sure the customers were satisfied with the service and the food," Mom added.

"When I saw Ava again, I called her over, and we began to talk, and I asked her out," Greg continued.

"And the rest, as they say, is history," my mother said, putting her other hand on top of Greg's.

Knowing my mom, that was the end of the story for her, but not for Jonathan, who cleared his throat and looked pointedly at Michelle, signaling loudly and clearly that he wanted her to finish up her assignment.

"That's such an interesting job," Michelle said. My mom and I flinched at the word *interesting*, both of us clearly remembering loathsome Lenore and her weaponized barrage of "interestings."

"Did you study commerce and business management at college?"

My mom hadn't graduated from high school, being pregnant with me at the time. Years later, she did get her high school degree by taking night courses, and she also took courses in restaurant management. Between her studies, work, and social life, she didn't have as much time as she would have wanted for being with me. Fortunately, very fortunately for me, we had Grandy and Aunt Debbie ready, willing, and eager to help out. As Grandy would say, I got a bargain deal, three moms for the price of one.

"No university degree, but I did take management courses at the community college," my mom said, her voice getting all whispery, as it did when she was embarrassed.

"Ava did it the old-fashioned way," Greg announced. "She worked her way up, job by job, and she should be proud of her accomplishments. I am."

And that was the truth, not B.S. to shut up Jonathan and Michelle. I had to give Greg that much, he was not a snob. He believed in hard work and bettering yourself. His father had owned a hardware store, and Greg had done construction work (hard to imagine, but true all the same) to earn the money for medical school.

"I'd love to hear more," Michelle simpered.

If Michelle wanted to hear more, she was going to hear more about the casino until it was coming out of her ears. I had done plenty of school presentations and speeches on it for social studies projects and English composition class.

"Casino Rama, which opened in 1996, is the only casino run by the First Nations in Canada, and has three thousand, seven hundred people working there. Ninety thousand square feet in size, it has twenty-five hundred slot machines, a hundred and ten gaming tables where you can play poker, baccarat, blackjack, craps, or roulette, ten restaurants, a five-thousand-seat entertainment center and a three-hundred-room hotel. Shall I book you a room there for a romantic weekend?" I asked sweetly. "I still have connections."

I looked over at Mom who appeared mortified by my spiel, and I felt terrible. I was only trying to help. Then Matt clapped and so did Greg, and she seemed to loosen up a bit.

It didn't take any time at all for Michelle and Jonathan to prick that little bubble of happiness. "Did your father work at the casino too? It must be a chore for him to travel to Toronto to see you," Michelle whipped in.

I hadn't seen that coming. I glanced around the restaurant as if somewhere on the walls some half-decent lying answer was hanging there, waiting to be discovered. I couldn't even glance at my mom.

"That's enough, Michelle. You're as a subtle as a drill," Matt said abruptly. "Although it is your turn to be under the microscope, I don't care to know anything more about you than I already do."

Matt had saved the day – again. Even Greg looked thankful.

One big unhappy family. Too bad there wasn't a photographer around to snap this portrait.

chapter seven

Off blisteringly tight ballet flats! Off stick-to-the-legs pantyhose! Off itchy pleated skirt! Off sneeze-inducing cashmere sweater! One by one, I tossed them onto my bed and then changed quickly and happily into jean shorts, a white T-shirt, sweat socks, and running shoes.

The next session at the photo studio had been canceled. Greg, who was on call this weekend, had been summoned to the hospital to do an emergency heart bypass. My mom made an appointment to get her and Elspeth's wisps of hair trimmed. And as soon as I found my bike helmet, I would be off on my Tour de Forest Hill route.

Where was it? I usually stored it on the top shelf in my closet, but it wasn't there. I turned on the TV and switched to a local news station, waiting to hear the weather report. I searched under the piles of clothing, the closet again, and under the bed. No helmet. I cursed as I banged my head on the bed frame.

Could have used that helmet now!

I sat down on the floor and watched the news for a bit. There was a report on a rash of home invasions and burglaries. I guess summertime was peak season for criminals – all those people on vacation leaving all those unoccupied houses. Easy pickings.

I was about to click off the TV when I saw video footage of a house that looked familiar. It was a total mess. The couch had been slashed open, the lamps broken, and stuff strewn all over the place.

"The owner, Leah Tomblin, an elderly woman who lives alone, evidently struggled with burglars," the news anchor said. "A neighbor walking his dog noticed that the front door was wide open and went inside to check. He found the victim unconscious in the front hallway and called the police. Leah Tomblin remains unconscious and is listed in serious but stable condition."

Mrs. Tomblin! Jeez! What was she doing home? She was supposed to have gone away for the weekend for the wedding of her cousin Linda Kennison's daughter. I turned off the TV and went to my computer, searching the station's website to see if they had any more information about the burglary. Nothing. Only additional video of Mrs. Tomblin's trashed living room.

I sat there staring at the monitor as I replayed the video. I had been in the house several times, the last time only two days ago. I had helped Mrs. Tomblin sort through her possessions and pack. She had been pretty low about leaving the house and about having to sell off things that had meant so much to her. Most of all, although she didn't say it, she was upset about moving into a retirement home.

I punched the desk. The few things she had left and wanted to take with her...I hoped they weren't all gone. Had the burglars wrecked the house because there wasn't much of any value to steal? All she had left were ancient electronics and kitchen appliances – a VCR, a twenty-inch color television, record and cassette players, an old microwave, an even older toaster oven, a coffee percolator, tea kettle, and blender – items that even at garage sale bargain prices no one had wanted to buy.

I supposed she might have had valuable jewelry stashed away. Had she been trying to hang on to those valuables? Was that why she'd fought the burglars?

None of this made any sense to me. However, it might to Yuri. After all, she was the crime expert. I e-mailed her, briefly outlining what had happened, and asked what she thought.

Crossing my fingers that Yuri would retrieve the e-mail sooner rather than later, I did a Google search for the numbers and addresses of the hospitals in the area, and started calling the nearest ones first to locate Mrs. Tomblin.

By the time I had called two hospitals (with no luck), Yuri had replied. She wrote that the burglary seemed like it had be done by amateurs – kids most likely, who had trashed the place because there was really nothing worth stealing. Professional burglars were, after all, professional. Their only aim was to get the goods and get out. They wouldn't wreck a place because they might leave fingerprints and DNA evidence. Plus, it would lengthen the amount of time they were in the premises. As a rule, pros weren't violent types either. Did Mrs. Tomblin own anything a professional burglar might know about and target?

I sat back again. I could tell from Yuri's e-mail that she was as excited about figuring out the burglary as she was about our contest to uncover the murderer in *The Body in the Library*. It wasn't real to her as it was to me. Real and really depressing. Right now, I just wanted to figure out where Mrs. Tomblin was and how she was doing.

chapter eight

Mrs. Tomblin was a patient at Toronto General Hospital. She had regained consciousness, hallelujah, and had been moved out of the ICU to a step-down unit. She was still too weak and dizzy to get out of bed. I knew all this because for the last three days I'd been going to the hospital every afternoon to check on her, wanting to visit with her. Each time she'd been either out of the room, undergoing yet another medical test, or sleeping.

This morning when I called, one of the nurses told me Mrs. Tomblin was up to seeing visitors, so I was heading off to see her after lunch. I wanted to get her flowers and chocolate treats – she really loved her sweets – so on my Tour de Forest Hill, I took a detour and went north. While my legs were pumping away at the pedals, my brain was on overdrive.

The nurse had told me that Mrs. Tomblin's condition was improving, which was good to hear, but she hadn't been in the greatest shape to begin with. I worried that her injuries would make her even more easily confused. Okay, she was going to be living in a retirement home with staff to look after her, but Mrs. Tomblin, like the rest of us, wanted to be able to do things herself and get around on her own. That was a major reason she was so unhappy about moving to the home.

Nothing about the burglary made sense. I kept checking the news channel and its website to see if there had been any progress in the case, but the story had already been shuffled off into their archives.

Yuri had found out which police division covered Mrs. Tomblin's neighborhood. She sent me messages telling me to go to the police and find out what was going on with the investigation. Like they were going to tell me! Yuri said I should pretend I worked for the school newspaper and was doing a story on it. I texted her back saying that she'd been reading too many mysteries. That story might have flown during the school year, but in the summer? Plus, why would a school newspaper do a story on a burglary?

Yuri insisted that it was important for Mrs. Tomblin's safety to figure it out. If the burglary had been done by kids or amateurs, it was done and over with. However, if the burglars had targeted her home to steal something specific that they hadn't found, she might still be in danger.

After thinking that over, I had to admit maybe Yuri hadn't been reading too many mysteries after all. I called Matt to run Yuri's theories past him and got his voicemail. I'd forgotten that he'd left yesterday for a week's vacation in the Maritimes.

I called Grandy and then felt even more worried because she

said that Yuri's theories had something to them. Great. That was exactly what I didn't want to hear.

Double great! I had just zoomed past the florist and almost veered into a car in the middle of my quick U-turn. The fancy chocolates for Mrs. Tomblin flew up and smash-landed on the road. I braked and bent over to pick up the box. Triple great! Once I'd bought flowers, I'd have to go back and buy another box.

Panting, I pedaled slowly toward the florist. I had chosen this florist because Greg got all his floral arrangements here, so they had to be good. As an added bonus, it was across the street from Max's Marketplace. Lovesick me was hoping like anything to see Colin again. That talk with him had me fantasizing about him more than ever, but I wasn't one bit less jumpy about seeing him.

How well did he know Mrs. Tomblin? I suppose I could ask him if I ever saw him again, and if I ever had the nerve to ask him anything. As I crouched down to lock up my bike, I heard my name.

"Phoebe, Phoebe!"

I stood up, my legs feeling wobbly, and turned around. Colin was waving at me to come over. I waited for the traffic to clear then dashed across the street.

"Hi," I said, out of breath.

"You would think from all that bike riding you'd be in better shape," he teased.

"I am in good shape," I panted. What was I going to say? That I couldn't breathe normally because he was standing so close to me? Yeah, right!

He gave me a quick glance. "You are in good shape," he said, blushing bright red when he realized what he'd said. "I saw you once playing field hockey. You were blasting up the field, stick-handling the ball right past the other team's players."

Now it was me blushing. Had Colin been watching me like I'd been watching him? Secretly stalking me like I was not-so-secretly stalking him? In my dreams. Nice dream, though he *had* noticed me. Twice. Maybe that was only because I had such a big mouth. I'd been yelling out to a couple of classmates to be my guards as I stick-handled the ball. But he did seem to like my big mouth. What a romantic suck I was turning out to be.

"Did you hear about Mrs. Tomblin?" he asked.

"I was just going to ask you that," I said.

"Do you mind?" He pointed to the cart of fruit and veg-etables beside him. "I have to restock."

Like I minded. I was standing close to him. I was talking to him. He was talking to me.

As he restocked the apples, then pears, peaches, and toma-toes, he told me that Mrs. Tomblin was a regular customer at Max's. When some of the other staff had gotten frustrated with her for forgetting what was in which aisle and what she had to buy, Colin had offered to do her shopping. Every week this month she'd brought in a list, and Colin had done her shopping and afterward had hailed a cab for her.

"She has her good and bad days," Colin said, standing still for a moment as he studied the fruit and vegetable display. "Oh," he said, flushing again when he caught me staring at him staring at the display. I had been staring at him the whole time, but he didn't need to know that. "I'm just checking to make sure they're lined up, otherwise, they roll off and onto the ground."

"I know," I said. "I've been attacked by an avalanche of apples a couple of times at the supermarket. You grab one, and all the others start rolling like crazy toward you and the floor. I guess whoever stacks the fruit there isn't as careful as you."

Way to go, girl! Complimenting him on his stacking ability. I looked away, then back at him. He did seem pleased, though. For someone who was as terrific at public speaking and debating as he was, it was astonishing how shy he was. We both went silent. I was all tongue-tied because I didn't want to say anything idiotic. Suddenly everything I had to say seemed silly.

"Did you see that article about Mrs. Tomblin and the burglary in *The Globe and Mail*?" he asked. "Is that how you found out?"

I shook my head and felt my face get hot again. "I saw it on the TV news." I didn't read *The Globe and Mail*, even though it was delivered every morning.

Naturally Colin did. I felt dumb beside him. "I'm kind of surprised that it would be in the newspaper. Doesn't *The Globe* mostly cover national and international stories?"

I felt like a big fraud, making it appear as if I knew this from my reading of the paper. Greg was always complaining about how little attention the newspaper paid to what was happening in Toronto – that's how I knew.

"Mrs. Tomblin is the niece of Rachel Malick, a famous photographer. Her aunt made Mrs. Tomblin the trustee of her collection, and Mrs. Tomblin has donated most of it to the Art Gallery of Ontario. They had an exhibition of Rachel Malick's photos just last month."

Mrs. Tomblin mentioned her aunt a lot. But she had never said she was famous.

"You're wondering how I know that," Colin said, stammering a bit as though he assumed I thought he was showing off. "I like taking photos. My da got me a digital camera a year ago, so I'd been studying how other photographers shoot their photos. Not like I'm good or anything, but I like it…."

I bet you are. I bet you're good at everything, I thought, but I wasn't about to say that while batting my eyelashes like some romance heroine. So once again, my big mouth had nothing it could say out loud.

"What are you up to next?" Colin asked.

I pointed to the florist shop. "I was going to buy flowers and take them to Mrs. Tomblin in the hospital. Chocolates too. I already bought a box, but it fell out of my basket."

"Mrs. Tomblin always buys Max's chocolate brownies. I could get those to give her. If you don't mind waiting an hour until my shift is over, I can come with you – if that's okay with you."

Okay wasn't the word. I nodded, thrilled almost speechless. "I'll get the flowers and wait for you in the parkette."

An hour never felt so long as I hung around feeling all fluttery to soon be – in a big stretch of the word – on a kind of a "date" with Colin. And all guilty for even thinking about Colin when I should be thinking about Mrs. Tomblin.

chapter nine

I paused in the doorway to Mrs. Tomblin's room, shocked by how punched up she was. She had a black eye with stitches above it, and cuts and bruises all over her arms. Had she been so thin before?

Yet that frail-looking person with the skinny arms had been strong enough to put up a fight and defend both herself and whatever it was the burglars had wanted to take from her.

"Hey Mrs. Tomblin," I said softly. Suddenly, I didn't know what to say or do and worried that she might not remember me. She opened her eyes, and on her face for a moment was that blank, frightened expression I'd seen before. She didn't remember me and it was scaring her.

Colin stepped forward. "Mrs. Tomblin, it's Colin, and I've got those chocolate fudge brownies you're always buying at Max's, and a package of Earl Grey tea, brown sugar, and a pint of cream."

"Colin…from Max's, please come in," she said, sounding relieved to be able to recognize Colin. "And…Phoebe, too, with such pretty flowers. Yes, Phoebe, Phoebe…the one who likes Agatha Christie mysteries."

Colin went over to Mrs. Tomblin's bedside. "I should have brought a steak too…for that eye. But my ma says a tea bag soaked in warm water over the eye is a cure-all. Can I give it a try?"

Mrs. Tomblin nodded, and I went off to the nursing station to get a pot of hot water for the tea and a vase for the flowers. When I returned, a police officer was in the room, too, holding a notepad in his hand.

"Constable Murdoch," Colin said, "this is Phoebe Hecht." The officer was beefy and red in the face from the heat outside. Colin continued, "Constable Murdoch is here to interview Mrs. Tomblin about the burglary."

"Think *this time* you can remember what happened?" Constable Murdoch sighed, clearly having lost his patience, no doubt after several going-nowhere interviews with her about the burglary.

That familiar frightened, blank expression was back on Mrs. Tomblin's face as she gazed at the constable. I knew if the case was to be solved, he had to get some information from her. And it seemed as if he was going to fail again.

I knew from experience – even liking Mrs. Tomblin as much as I did – that it was easy, way too easy, to lose patience with her forgetfulness. Yet, if the constable didn't ease up, he'd never get anything out of her.

"The burglary…." she said faintly.

"The *burglary* that occurred while you were at home last Friday night."

"The policeman is trying to help you, Mrs. Tomblin," I interrupted. I had to persuade her of that so she would be able to remember. She looked up at me, then over at the constable, her expression still perplexed.

He muttered something under his breath. "You must have heard something because you woke up. Did you hear voices? Do you remember how many? What did you see when you went downstairs? Did you fight them? Or did they grab you?"

Mrs. Tomblin peeked over at me, then Colin, as if somehow we'd be able to answer for her.

"You don't remember anything, do you?" he said, shaking his head.

"No, I don't," she whispered, shutting her eyes. She looked so bewildered and frightened, I wanted to cry. The constable patted down his various pockets searching for a card. He found one and held it out. I took it.

"I will give you a call when you return home." Then to me he said, "When she is feeling stronger, see if you can get a list of what was stolen. When she goes room to room, she'll see what's missing."

Also being back home might help her remember more about what happened, but I didn't want to say that in case it didn't. The experience might have been so awful that she had buried it permanently.

"Right." He was about to close his notepad when he noticed something in it. "Where's her next of kin?" he asked, not even bothering now to ask Mrs. Tomblin directly. "Her son…Richard Tomblin. He's not around?"

"He's on vacation," I said, not sure whether he was or wasn't.

"I'll be there…to help when you come," I told him. "I'll call when it's a good time. I have your card."

"Right." He muttered good-bye, looking relieved to be going, and, I bet, not looking forward to having to go through this all again.

Mrs. Tomblin sank back into the bed.

"I can get a cup of tea ready for you and those brownies you love," Colin said. She opened her eyes and Colin helped her sit up, then made the tea and brought her a plate with brownies. As she ate, he told her a story about his father.

"My da, he's a super at one of those small rental apartments near Avenue Road. The kitchen sink in one apartment got plugged up, and my da goes in with his plumbing gear to clean the drain. The man who lives there, he has a cat, and Da, he hates cats, and this cat, my da swears, knows it. So after the job is finished, the man insists on my da having a beer with him. It's the end of the day, so Da agrees. He stands leaning against the counter, and the man then insists that he sit. My da doesn't want to sit because he knows what's coming if he sits. But to be polite and all, he sits, and the second he's seated, the cat speeds out of the living room, leaps right into my da's lap, turns over onto his back, and looks up at him. The man says he's amazed. 'Felix, he doesn't do that with anyone but you,' he says. 'He's particular about who he likes, and I can see he likes you.' From the way the cat is looking up at my da and hissing, Da knows it's not that the cat likes him. The cat knows Da hates him, and he does this to torture my da for not liking cats."

I couldn't recall ever seeing Mrs. Tomblin laugh, but she did, a weak laugh, but a laugh all the same. "Cats, I don't like them myself," she admitted. "My late husband, he did though. We had two cats, Mallory and Malone."

Listening to Colin talk, I envied his having a good, loving dad. I envied him for not being ashamed at all that his dad was a super. Not that he should be, or that I would be. I wasn't ashamed of my past, but my mom's shame made it hard for me to talk about it without feeling like I was betraying her somehow. Her shame was staining my happy memories.

I half listened as Mrs. Tomblin related how attached Mallory and Malone, a pair of brown mackerel tabbies, were to her husband. The story was super detailed, like all her stories about the past. So detailed that I could picture Mallory and Malone right from their peppered noses to the *M* pattern on their foreheads and their white sock paws as if they were right in front of me ready to pounce, all seventeen pounds of each of them, into my lap. It was good to see her pick up and remember something that made her cheerful.

Colin leaned close, listening intently. I had liked him a lot, even before I knew him. Sometimes, people you think you will like turn out to be people you don't like much, once you get to know them. But I liked Colin even more than I had before. Way more. And now I could look at him as much as I wanted to without having to stalk him on my bike.

As they continued to talk I went through the get-well cards Mrs. Tomblin had received from her friends and neighbors. I was relieved that she had received cards and bouquets of flowers other than mine. It was good to know that she wasn't all alone. I wondered if she could count on any of these people to take care of her…if she needed them. That was what really mattered. There was no card from her son, Richard, who was still missing in action. Did he know? And if he did, did he care at all?

chapter ten

Glass of milk. Check. Strawberry cereal bar. Check. Banana. Check. Piece of paper with scribbled questions to ask Yuri. Check. Computer on. Check. So where was Yuri? I had my breakfast to snack on while she answered my questions about Mrs. Tomblin. We'd set up this time yesterday to IM each other.

Mrs. Tomblin was going to be released from the hospital tomorrow. Therefore, it was urgent that we figure out – how about *try* to figure out – whether or not the burglars were planning to return to finish the job. Of course, they could have returned to finish the job while she was in the hospital. But what if she had hidden away something they were after and that was why they beat her up – to find out where it was hidden? If Yuri and I could figure out something about the burglary, it might also be useful in prodding Mrs. Tomblin's memory, so the police could solve the case.

I drank down the milk, gobbled up the cereal bar, and was

about to take a bite of banana when I heard a ping signaling a message from Yuri.

Dear Miss Hecht, the Toronto Miss Marple:
Sorry, sorry, and sorry again. I was teaching my little sister to ride her bike and no can do. Need your expertise. She doesn't want me to let go of the bike yet. Human training wheels, that's what I am and bruised ones too.

So shoot your questions at me. I'm ready.

Dear Miss Kimura, the Tokyo Miss Marple:
One piece of bike advice. Hold on to your sister's bike from behind, not from the side. Then you can let go without her freaking out, and she'll see she can ride without human training wheels.

Excellent. Will do.

Yesterday, you great woman of mystery detection, you solved the mystery of *The Body in The Library.* How did you know – not even halfway through the story – that the widower son-in-law and his girlfriend did it? I raced to finish the book to see if you had guessed right. Right up to almost the end I still kept believing it was the producer. I know, I know, you have to look at the evidence and suspects objectively. I know, I know, you have to let the evidence lead you, instead of leading the evidence in the direction you want it to go.

I promise to try to do that with Mrs. Tomblin's case. So here it is for you to solve.

Typing like a demon, I told Yuri everything I knew up to now about the case and Mrs. Tomblin. I pressed Send and finished the banana while waiting for Yuri to think everything through.

Phoebe,
From all you've told me about Mrs. Tomblin, it seems as if she could be in the early stage of Alzheimer's disease. My great-auntie has it, and that was what she was like, too, at the start.

That was what I had been thinking, actually fearing, not that I knew very much more than it was a brain disease that eventually left older people unable to recognize their families, or remember how to eat or walk or do anything on their own. Maybe Yuri was wrong, and maybe I was wrong, but Mrs. Tomblin was exhibiting all the early symptoms. I felt so sorry for her, especially because it seemed she didn't have many people who would be around to take care of her when she got worse, other than the staff at the retirement home.

Yuri,
Let's say Mrs. Tomblin has it, how can I help her to remember what happened, at least a bit? Or is that a lost cause?

Phoebe,
Not at all. Keep on doing what you have been doing. She might remember more once she's at home and feeling safe. You already have seen that she's better during the day and worse at night. Ask her questions about the burglary in the morning. From what you've told me she obviously likes and trusts you, so maybe you can get her to remember more about what happened.

Okay. Will do. You got that list ready of things I should be investigating at the house to assess whether the burglary was a crime of opportunity or planned in advance?

Crime of opportunity, excellent! You're getting the lingo.

I got the lingo, you got the detective skills.

You're always underestimating yourself! Drives me nuts! Wait till you've read as many mysteries as I have and you'll be seeing clues and crimes and criminals everywhere. (This makes my parents berserk!)

Here's what you have to investigate.

How the burglars got into the house. If the lock was jim-mied, it was pros. If a window or door was broken, it was amateurs.

Pros don't like to break into a house when the owners are there. They watch the house to see when the coast is clear. Amateurs are reckless, sloppy. Are there bars or hangouts in the area? Could be some kids got drunk or high and Mrs. Tomblin's was the nearest or easiest place to break into.

Stop, I've got to break in. Yuck, I didn't mean to pun. Mrs. Tomblin was supposed to be away for the weekend. So it could have been pros. I have to find out from her, if she can remember, who knew she was going away.

But the house was totaled, and like you told me, pros like to grab what they came for and get out pronto. So maybe it was amateurs who trashed the house because they were pissed off since there wasn't much to steal. And when Mrs. Tomblin sur-prised them, they panicked and fought her.

But what if they were pros and were afraid of being caught and convicted if Mrs. Tomblin was able to identify them? They are not usually violent though, right? And aren't they usually disguised with ski masks and don't they wear gloves so they won't leave fingerprints?

Way to go, Miss Toronto Jane Marple! I knew you had more of her in you than you *knew.*

I was flattered for a second, and excited, I had to admit, getting as caught up as Yuri was in the game of figuring out what happened. Then, when I remembered this was *real* and how bruised and beaten up Mrs. Tomblin was, and how wrecked her house was, my excitement instantly evaporated, and I was back to being worried and scared for Mrs. Tomblin. I had to figure this out to keep her safe.

Hello! Taking a timeout already, Phoebe?

No, I was just thinking. What else?

When you go back inside Mrs. Tomblin's house, see if there are any valuables out in the open that weren't stolen, and ask her if she has any valuables hidden away, and if anyone knew she had them in the house. That'll help you figure out whether the burglars were pros looking for something specific, or amateurs who grabbed whatever they could carry.

Okay. I told the constable investigating the case I would help Mrs. Tomblin make a list of what was stolen. Her insurance company probably will need a list too.

Good luck detecting. Gotta go. My sister is waiting for the rest of her bike lesson. Hope she will ride off into the sunset without me hanging on to the bike. Human kite instead of human training wheels. Wish me luck.

Wish me luck too.

And tons of it. Because I was going to need it. I was suddenly feeling not at all capable of uncovering anything worth uncovering.

chapter eleven

I stood in front of Mrs. Tomblin's house, a box of nut and caramel chocolates in my knapsack, a notepad and pen in my
hands, ready (or not) to do some sleuthing. After getting that
checklist from Yuri, I'd read several articles on Alzheimer's disease on the Internet.

As Yuri had told me, the memories of people who were in
the early stages of the disease got worse as the day went on. So
I'd gotten up at six in the morning, done my Tour de Forest Hill,
and had arrived at Mrs. Tomblin's by ten. We'd made plans to
start an inventory list of what had been stolen or damaged for
the police and her insurance company.

Outside the house, I was going to do my own inventory of
clues. I'd also done Google sleuthing on burglary techniques
and investigation methods on several police websites (advising,
it seemed to me, not only new-to-the-job police officers, but
new-to-the-job burglars) and mystery writers' message boards

that passed along crime detection tips and strategies to fellow authors.

I wanted to survey the outside of the house for the burglars' point of entry before I went in to visit, and before the clues, if there were any, were washed away by the thunderstorm predicted for later in the day.

I circled the front of the house, not expecting to see anything out of the ordinary. Even amateurs would know that it was smarter to break in from the back than the front because you had less chance of being seen.

In the backyard I noticed a cellar window had been broken and was boarded up. I went over and knelt down at the edge of the flower bed next to the window. That was strange. There were no footprints in the soil and none of the flowers had been trampled. If the burglars had broken in through the window, they would have crushed a couple of flowers. I felt something on my knee. I looked down – a large shard of glass. There were several large shards. Weird. If the burglars had broken the glass to get in, the largest pieces of glass should have fallen into the basement. Only if the window had been broken from the inside would larger pieces scatter in the yard like this.

Then I checked out the lock on the back porch door with a magnifying glass I'd borrowed from Greg. There were lots of little scratches and nicks around the lock, as though it had been picked, but there was no damage to the door. That was the mark of a pro. So why break a window when you already had opened the back door? Had it been broken for show to make the police think it was amateurs when it was really pros? Why even go to the trouble? None of this made sense…yet. I'd text Yuri later about this to see what she could come up with.

I went back around the house and knocked on the front door.

"Phoebe, how nice it is to see you," Mrs. Tomblin said, all cheery. As she stepped aside to let me in, she almost stumbled. Good thing she was behind me because my face must have broadcast my shock and dismay.

To my non-medical eyes, she didn't appear to be in good enough shape to have been sent home. She had a brace on one knee and had difficulty walking, even with the aid of a cane. The slash above her eye had become infected and was oozing and swollen. Thank goodness home care nurses were assigned to look in on her every day until she moved into the retirement home because she sure still needed care.

The living room was a disaster zone. Everything was all over the place. The oil paintings were hanging crookedly on the walls, some of them slashed. The floor and carpet were littered with pieces of shattered vases, china, and lamps. The coffee table was overturned, and the legs broken on the end tables. Even the couch cushions had been cut and the stuffing pulled out.

To look at it all, you had to think amateurs or kids had done this. No pro would waste energy and time on making this unholy mess…unless they got a big charge out of doing it and beating up old ladies.

It almost seemed as though it had been done for show. I mean everything, every single piece of furniture, had been wrecked. When I got angry enough to toss stuff, I tossed whatever was closest or whatever I saw first. This seemed methodical, in a weird way, as methodical as some play director arranging a stage set. But I could be wrong. If kids were high on meth or something, they'd have enough of a major boost of crazy-mean energy to do something like this. Still….

"The police said not to clean up yet because I might clean up evidence," Mrs. Tomblin said, waving her hand toward the living room. True, but with a cane in one hand and a brace on one leg, it would be dangerous enough for her to get around safely in the best of conditions. With the living room now an obstacle course, it would be near impossible for Mrs. Tomblin not to injure herself some more. Jeez.

"Here, I have something for you," I said, twisting to pull the gold box of chocolates out of my knapsack.

"Chocolates!" Mrs. Tomblin said, all excited like a little kid. "Do you think I can have a few now? I just had my breakfast."

"It's always chocolate time," I said. "I just had my breakfast, and I wouldn't mind a piece either."

Holding onto Mrs. Tomblin's arm, I walked her over to the kitchen, which looked basically untouched, except for a few missing appliances. What variety of burglar took a decrepit blender and a toaster oven? The more I saw, the more confused I was.

I placed the box on the table and we sat down, choosing our favorite chocolates to munch on. When I got up to make a pot of tea, I tried to turn the conversation to the inventory, but my attempts were futile. Mrs. Tomblin was all caught up in telling me the story of how she and her husband had chosen this house forty-five years ago.

The doorbell rang. Rang wasn't the word. Insistent, nonstop ringing was what it was. Presuming the finger on the ringer belonged to Constable Murdoch, who likely wanted to get in fast, in order to get out fast. I got up and helped Mrs. Tomblin rise.

"We're coming!" I shouted, like he could hear. He might hear if he would take his lousy finger off the doorbell. With Mrs. Tomblin clutching me tightly, we walked slowly to the front door. As I scowled at him, he lifted his finger off the bell.

"I thought you didn't hear!"

"Mrs. Tomblin can't walk fast. She has a brace and cane, okay?" I snapped, then immediately regretted it. As usual. "Come in," I said.

I settled Mrs. Tomblin into a wingchair in the living room, and Constable Murdoch grabbed a dining room chair. "We were indulging ourselves in some chocolates. Care for one?" Mrs. Tomblin asked the constable.

He muttered under his breath. Taking that for a yes, I went to get the box. I was about to take it in when I decided I would choose the most gooey, chewy, stick-to-your-teeth-and-roof-of-your-mouth ones, and put them on a plate. Hopefully, that would limit his ability to mutter a stream of frustrated comments about Mrs. Tomblin.

I offered him the pecan caramels and almond pralines.

"They're special chocolates. Delicious," Mrs. Tomblin said.

He eyeballed them for a moment as though he were weighing whether they were too girly for him to eat. He couldn't resist, though, and gobbled down two. That gave us a few minutes' reprieve as his cheek did the Twist in an effort to get the caramel and nuts off his teeth.

"Can we start with what is missing? We can't arrest the burglars without knowing what they stole." The constable spoke every word loudly, clearly, slowly. It would be nice to think it was because of the chocolate, but it seemed to me (and from the wounded expression on Mrs. Tomblin's face, it must have seemed to her too) that it was because the constable considered her not only deaf, but dumb.

She began to look frantically around the living room. "The... pictures are gone."

"Pictures gone," he repeated. "What type of pictures? Paintings? Watercolors? Family photos?"

"Yes, my family photos...they are gone."

"How many?" He swallowed hard, as if he were gulping down a burst of frustration and irritation. "What did they look like?"

I knew Mrs. Tomblin wasn't being much help, and that he was just trying to do his job. But that didn't excuse his being rude and impatient. Making someone feel stupid didn't snap them out of their supposed stupidity – a lesson Constable Murdoch and a few of my teachers at Dunvegan had yet to learn. Making me feel stupid certainly hadn't propelled the right answers out of me in class.

I was feeling almost as flustered as Mrs. Tomblin – intimidated, stupid, my mind blanking out, too. I made myself slowly study the living room. Eventually I was able to clearly picture everything as it had been before. I glanced over at the wall next to the staircase. The paint was brighter in six distinct rectangles. "Mrs. Tomblin is referring to the framed black-and-white photographs that were hanging right there. Her aunt was a famous photographer."

"You think you could tell me the name of the *famous*

photographer and what was in the photos? That might be of use," he said brusquely.

I resisted my first impulse to give him the finger. I resisted my second impulse to sulk and clam up. I didn't say anything until I could see the pictures vividly enough to describe them. "The photos show kids playing and people hanging around on main streets in downtown Toronto in the forties and fifties. The street signs are in the pictures – Bathurst and Bloor, Vaughan and St. Clair."

"The *famous* photographer, whose name is…?"

Mrs. Tomblin was silent during all this. Silent, in that she wasn't speaking out loud; her lips though, were moving as if she was speaking to herself.

"The aunt's name is…" *Come to me, come to me, work, memory, work.* "…Rachel Malick."

"Yes, Rachel Malick, she was my aunt. Aunt Rachel," Mrs. Tomblin said proudly.

"The *famous* Rachel Malick," he said. "I never heard of her. Famous like Vincent van Gogh, huh?"

"Famous enough," I said. Like I knew. I'd never heard of her either, before speaking with Colin. That didn't count for much, since I hadn't even known photographers could be famous. Painters yes, but photographers? "Other things were taken. You think you could write them down? There used to be a VCR over there on the television stand. And a TV, too, a twenty-inch Sony Trinitron. And on that end table, a Panasonic portable phone."

Was there something else? I looked around. No. "Why take them? Why bother stealing an ancient VCR, worth maybe ten bucks, if you were lucky, and an even more ancient TV, and a portable phone that was huge and outdated? Everything had to be a decade old, at least. Not big-ticket items, even to start with."

"Kids, that's why. They'll steal anything," the Constable said with authority.

Kids. Yeah sure. Kids knew electronics, knew what was a big-ticket item, what was hot. No kids would bother stealing electronics ready for the junkyard or some museum. I didn't say any of that, though. The constable was just trying to do his job, I reminded myself.

Mrs. Tomblin remained a silent bystander, as if this weren't her living room and these weren't her things being discussed. She kept glancing over at me, kind of like a toddler glances at her mother, wanting me to take charge, to take care of things.

"Anything else?" he asked.

"Mrs. Tomblin had a set of sterling silver cutlery. Worth thousands, she told me. It was stored in the top drawer of the dining room buffet." I rushed over and yanked the drawer open. The set was still there.

A ten-dollar VCR likely near my age was stolen, but a silver cutlery set worth thousands was left behind. "Some things were taken from the kitchen," I said, and the Constable and Mrs. Tomblin followed me there. "A toaster oven and a blender."

The constable groaned. "Kids, didn't I tell you? They'll take anything."

This was too bizarre. It had to have been staged. I knew kids could do anything if they were high, but really. This stuff? Nobody would want it. Nobody had wanted it at the garage sale.

I had to get him off the kids theory. Out of the blue it hit me how to do that. "Let's go upstairs to Mrs. Tomblin's bedroom,"

I said. At the top of the stairs, I turned to face him. "I'll show you why I think it wasn't kids." Then I faced Mrs. Tomblin. "Is it alright if I open up the top drawer on your night table?"

She nodded yes.

"If I were a kid looking to grab cash and stuff to fence for drugs or whatever, I wouldn't leave without checking out the night table drawer. My grandmother and aunt keep their spare cash and jewelry in that drawer. Lots of people do."

I rushed forward and yanked open the drawer. Inside I found a large embroidered velvet bag full of jewelry and handed it to him.

He laid out the items in the bag.

Before my mom married Greg, I'd never seen a big diamond. The diamonds in Grandy's ring were tiny. Aunt Debbie's former husband hadn't even given her a ring. Lucky to get a wedding band and license out of that one, she always joked. The square-shaped diamond solitaire in Mrs. Tomblin's ring looked to be several carats, not as humungous as the one Greg had given my mother, but pretty darn close. And her wedding band was ringed with fair-sized diamonds too. There was also an emerald ring set in diamonds, a triple-strand pearl choker, and pearl drop earrings.

"Kids…just getting in and out, didn't take the time to look here," he persisted.

I lost confidence in my deductions. The constable could be correct, and I could be wrong. Still, like my role model, Miss Marple (not saying I had her detecting skills by a long shot), I had to trust my instincts, and they were telling me there was more to this.

He handed the jewelry back to me, and I returned it to the drawer. As he was leaving, he reminded Mrs. Tomblin to give him a call if she remembered anything more, almost snickering when he said that, since it had been me who had done most of the remembering here.

After he shut the door, I stuck my tongue out. "I don't like him," I said.

"Me neither," she said, and got all wobbly. My heart went out to her. She'd been assaulted and robbed, and given the lack of evidence, it was likely going to be a cold case Constable Murdoch would file away soon.

Unless I came up with some clues for him to chase down.

chapter twelve

I was waiting for Colin at my tree, the maple with a canopy of leaves large enough to shade a patio and a gnarled trunk, made extra-gnarled by the names people had carved into it to remind whoever came to sit in the shade that they too once had sat here. Some of the names were so old-fashioned and faint that they must have been carved decades ago. Names like Dora and Eugenie and Hiram and Ralph were side by side with the ever-popular Brittany and Matthew.

Colin was going to join me for lunch during his noon break so we could discuss Mrs. Tomblin. In a way, she'd been our matchmaker. Not that we were an "us" (outside of my fantasies). It was more accurate to say that thanks to Mrs. Tomblin, I was talking and hanging out with Colin, rather than mooning over him and stalking him, hoping for something to happen. Mrs. Tomblin had been that something.

I wasn't much of a planner. My mother, on the other hand,

was a planner, to put it mildly. After having me unplanned by choices bad, worse, and terrible, she'd vowed to turn her life totally around. And the irony was that she'd finally achieved everything she'd dreamed of through a lucky chance meeting with Dr. Gregory Creighton in a place where there was so much loss and very little luck for most people.

So there had been chance and luck; mostly though, there had been hard, hard work and planning. It was no wonder that Michelle had asked my mom if she had a business degree. Mom had made a business plan for her life, and step by step, had accomplished it. I was glad for her. She had earned it. She deserved it. And she was terrified of losing it.

You would have thought, and I certainly did, that after nineteen months of marriage to Greg and having a baby with him, my mother would have eased up on her constant dread that eventually, inevitably, someone from her past was going to reveal something that somehow would ruin everything.

Case in point – what had gone down yesterday at lunch. Roz Chisholm, the wife of one of Greg's doctor friends, had come over to see Mom. She was on the board of a local food bank and wanted Mom's assistance managing and distributing the donations. I could tell Mom was flattered that her restaurant experience was regarded by Roz as being an important skill, and that the wife of a friend of Greg's was friendly, rather than patronizing.

I had tried to boost her confidence by telling stories that showed how my mom always handled things like a pro. She was super organized, great in a crisis, which was once or twice a day in the restaurant business, and tough but fair dealing with the staff and suppliers. All the same, I could see Mom growing more apprehensive, afraid that I was going to blurt out something that would humiliate her.

After Roz left, I vented. "Have I given you away yet? I'm not going to – ever! Have some faith in me, will you?"

"I'm sorry Phoebe, I really am," she said. "You know…" she shrugged, clearly embarrassed.

Okay, she was sorry, but her being sorry just wasn't cutting it with me anymore. Was she sorry that she acted the way she had, or sorry that the way she acted ticked me off? It was too much of the latter, and not nearly enough of the former, by my estimate.

"Phoebe, did you hear me? I'm sorry."

"I heard you," I said bitterly. "Why don't you show me how sorry you are by acting differently when Grandy, Aunt Debbie, and Adam are here tomorrow?"

They were arriving tonight and staying at a hotel. I was so excited about seeing them. I'd told Grandy about Mrs. Tomblin and Mrs. Tomblin about Grandy, and was going to introduce them. I was also nervous – to the max – after how Mom had behaved with Roz. She was probably nervous too, fearing some chance remark or story that would upset Greg.

I desperately wanted this visit to go well, and I was going to try my best to make sure everybody got along – even if it made me seem like one of those rinky-dink counselors on daytime talk shows.

"If I jump up and sing the national anthem do you think you might notice me?" Colin was teasing, but I was so startled I almost jumped up too. "You were thinking about Mrs. Tomblin, huh," he said, and sat down beside me on the blanket.

I nodded. I had been thinking of her – many thoughts ago. He was so close that we were touching shoulders, and I got all girly and swoony for a moment. I could smell his shampoo and something else.

"You're smelling the Limburger, Munster and aged Provolone cheese?" he asked, catching me sniffing. "Man, what a stink! And people eat them. Go figure. I was working behind the cheese counter. Prepare yourself; if there are any rodents around here, they're probably heading in this direction."

I laughed. And then he did too, shifting his shoulder even closer to mine. As we ate the lunch he'd brought for us (thankfully, ham on croissants, and not some stinky cheese), I brought him up to speed on what was going on with Mrs. Tomblin and the case.

"None of it makes any sense, period. What they stole, why they beat Mrs. Tomblin," Colin said. When he said the same thing that I had been thinking, I was pleased. No, actually ecstatic. The fact that we were leaning against each other comfortably like old friends contributed big time, too.

"I told my da and ma, and they don't think it adds up either."

At that, I felt a spike of envy again that he had a father and mother he was close to, that he could tell things to. Even though I had told all to Grandy, I couldn't tell my mom. Telling her would have meant explaining away or even having to lie more about what all my "friends" and I were doing this summer and how I got involved with Mrs. Tomblin.

"You've known Mrs. Tomblin for a while," I said. "Why doesn't her son cut his vacation short when she's been robbed and beaten up?"

I kept waiting for Mrs. Tomblin to mention her son in the hospital. She hadn't though. Once she was home, I had finally asked, and she'd told me he was on vacation in Italy and left it at that.

"I've met him. From what I could see, he isn't someone she can rely on," Colin said. "Once in a while he used to drive her over to Max's. He'd be picking away at her the whole time she was shopping, telling her how she was slow, how she could never find what she was looking for, barking at her to her hurry up. You get the picture."

That told me all I needed to know. About the son and Colin too. If it had been me describing that scene to Colin, I would have been cursing out the son. That wasn't Colin's style. He didn't get all fired up and hot like I did, not even about creeps. There was nothing more to be said about Mrs. Tomblin's son, so I moved on, wanting to get his opinion on Yuri's theories about the crime.

"Yuri's right," he said, sighing. "Mrs. Tomblin's house was targeted."

I sighed too, our sighs meaning the same thing. It was worse for Mrs. Tomblin if the house had been targeted because it still might be a target, and Mrs. Tomblin as well.

Colin sat up straighter, or at least tried to. His apron strings were caught on the gnarly bark.

"Sweet mother of mercy, you've got me in your fiendish grip," he joked, playing up his Irish accent.

"Don't squirm! Hold still, will you!" I giggled as I pulled on the strings. We faced each other, laughing, then stared — Colin's face just inches from mine. I thought for a second, and a wonderful one it was, that he might kiss me. He must have been considering it because his cheeks reddened as he moved his head closer. But he didn't.

Why he didn't he? Like I was going to make the first move. Yeah, sure. Not because of some silly girly dating rules about how it was better to be the one chased than the chaser. No. Because I knew how much I liked him that way, and I didn't know if that was the way he liked me.

"Thanks," he mumbled.

"About Mrs. Tomblin and the robbery and how she was targeted, what kind of target she was, how do we all figure all that out?" I asked, wanting to bring the conversation back to Mrs. Tomblin. "You know how trusting she can be."

He nodded. Mrs. Tomblin was too eager to be listened to, liked, taken care of.

"During the garage sale, she was letting people enter her house and use the powder room downstairs. Someone could have cased the place for a robbery," I said.

"And she told me she was going away for that weekend wedding," he added. "If she told me, she probably told her neighbors and even people at the garage sale. I bet you lots of people knew the house was going to be empty."

"Still," I wondered aloud, "if the burglars were experienced and just on the lookout for empty houses, why leave behind easy-to-snatch stuff like the expensive silverware and all that cash and jewelry?"

Colin kept nodding as I talked. "Exactly. The photographs! That's it!" He slapped his forehead. "You said Mrs. Tomblin kept going on to the cop about the photos being gone."

"Yeah, there were six black-and-white photos, maybe more; they were the ones I saw, hanging on the walls along the staircase. They were taken by her aunt."

"The photos must have been the target!" Colin said, his voice rising.

"The photos? Why steal them? Couldn't you just make new ones from the negatives?" I asked. Plus, and I didn't say this out loud, how much could they be worth? They were old black-and-white pictures of ordinary people doing everyday things.

"They are almost as famous as the photographs done by Yousuf Karsh," he answered. "You know, he's the Canadian photographer renown for his portraits of people like Albert Einstein and Winston Churchill. You must have seen reproductions of some of these pictures for sure. They're in our textbooks."

"Are Malick's as valuable?"

"Yeah, almost," he said, flooring me. "But I like Rachel Malick's better...way better."

"So do I! There's so much going on between the people that you catch, but don't quite understand."

"Absolutely, that's what makes them so great!" he said. "Malick was a master at capturing people in the midst of doing everyday things."

I nodded. In my opinion, people looked best when they weren't posed, when they looked like themselves. I was still baffled, though, by how any photograph could be as valuable as a painting. All you had to do was print the negative again if the camera was a film camera, and if it was a digital camera, you just had to upload the file from the memory card onto a computer and print out the image. So I asked Colin about this, hoping that the question didn't prove what a know-nothing I was.

"Wouldn't there be negatives for Rachel Malick's pictures? If you wanted another one, all you would have to do is make another print. So then why are old photographs so valuable?"

"Most of the old film photographers like Rachel Malick printed their own photographs, too," Colin said. "That way they had total control over how the photo appeared. They could crop it and focus in on just a part of the image on the negative, control the tones and shades, and make the print darker or lighter. Malick experimented a lot with the tones and the cropping of images, and she was excellent at it. The prints made from negatives at the time the photos were taken are the most expensive for collectors to buy. They're called vintage prints. Malick only made a few of each picture, numbered them, and signed them on the back. So part of what makes a famous photographer's picture valuable is how many prints were made originally from the negative. Most of Malick's prints, like most other black-and-white photos of the time, are silver gelatin prints. But since she was such an excellent printer, she also printed some on platinum paper. Platinum prints are amazing. There are as many shades and tones of black and white as there are hues on a color photo. Those platinum prints last as long as a piece of steel would – centuries. So you see, not all the prints from a single image are of equal value – artistically or in the marketplace."

He stopped, flushed, his face one big blotch of red, and looked over at me, then away. "I'm boring you. You think I'm a a conehead, a grind—"

"Cut it out!" I said. I couldn't believe he would think I

thought that. But at least it mattered to him what I thought of him. And it didn't give him time to focus on how much of a doofus I felt compared to him.

I knew Colin well enough to recognize that he wasn't lecturing me as if I were dumb or ignorant. But there was no doubt about it. Colin was a conehead and a grind – in the best possible way.

"So you think the burglars were after the photos?" I asked.

"Maybe," he said. "Remember I told you that recently the Art Gallery of Ontario had an exhibition of Malick's photographs and there was a feature article on her and Mrs. Tomblin in *The Globe and Mail*? The article said she had donated most of the photos to the AGO, keeping ten vintage prints and some mass-market reprints for sentimental reasons. I think she said she still had her aunt's negatives, contact prints, and proofs. Odd that she kept those."

Then it hit me that the photo Mrs. Tomblin had given me might be one of the numbered originals. I would check the back when I got home before I said anything about it to Colin. Maybe I wasn't the only person she had given photos to. Maybe they hadn't even been stolen, not all of them anyway.

Neither of us said what we both were probably thinking. If only we could ask Mrs. Tomblin about the photographs, and if only she could remember.

chapter thirteen

Everyone was on their best behavior. That meant that Grandy, Aunt Debbie, Mom, Greg, and I were – in person – as stiff, formal and unnatural as the Creighton family portraits Greg was showing off like a museum curator.

"My, my," Grandy said, with strained politeness. "Now *that's* a picture." She'd uttered a variation of that at every photo on the tour. Grandy had been relaxed at first, when we'd greeted each other in the front hallway. She'd dressed up in a pale yellow linen pantsuit. Her hair had been permed and cut, and she was even wearing lipstick and eye shadow. To me she looked wonderful, the pale yellow of her suit accenting her tan and freckles.

"Mother, don't you ever wear sunblock?" my mother asked almost immediately. She studied Grandy's face as though it were one big map of lines, creases, and brown spots. So what if it was? That was Grandy. If looking her age didn't bother Grandy, why should it bother my mother?

Mom was super conscious about keeping her skin snow white and unwrinkled. She always sat in the shade, wearing a high SPF sunblock and a huge hat.

"Yes I do, Ava, and a wide-brimmed hat too," she said, barely swallowing a sigh. "You know I love being outside as much as I can. I'd have to wear a suit of armor not to get tanned. Or sit in the house all day."

I saw Greg open his mouth. I hoped he wasn't going to give Grandy the same lecture he'd given me earlier this summer about skin cancer and how to recognize a mole that had turned cancerous. He'd even shared his medical text with photographs of cancerous moles. That had been a fun bonding exercise.

He meant well. But I liked being outside in the summer as much as Grandy did. Although I painted myself with all the various sunblocks Mom bought me for my face, lips, and body, I was nearly as tanned as Grandy.

Before Greg could lead us to the next grouping of family portraits, I grasped Grandy's hand and asked, "Can I show Grandy my new bike now?"

"Later," my mother said. "There are still some portraits we haven't seen yet."

"More photos," Aunt Debbie said, almost sighing.

She took one foot out of a sandal and wiggled her toes. Aunt Debbie was dressed up too. She was wearing cropped black pants, a sleeveless striped shirt and black wedge sandals. Her dark brown hair was short and curly like Grandy's, but it was naturally curly, and, she moaned, becoming naturally gray too.

Leaning close to me, she whispered, "If I had known I was going to be on a guided tour, I would have worn flats."

"It's almost over," I whispered back. "Only a few portraits to go."

She nodded wearily. "Not that I don't want to look at you, and Elspeth's a cutie, but…"

"My favorite," Greg said, stopping before the largest portrait. There we were in the middle of a spectacular garden with miniature Japanese maples on one side and a blossoming magnolia tree on the other. We sat, unsmiling, our posture perfect (Elspeth belted into straight posture by my mother's arms), on an antique wooden bench, lined up like kids waiting to be summoned into the principal's office.

"That's something else, isn't it?" Grandy finally said, digging deep to come up with a comment that could be a compliment. She wasn't much for telling white lies. Not like my mother, who had become an expert after years of soothing and satisfying unhappy staff and customers.

I glanced over at Mom who was gazing at the portrait. She couldn't possibly think it was good, or that we looked good, could she? It was hard to tell. My mother wasn't the easiest person to read. She seemed to be pleased. Pleased, I supposed, because the portraits captured her in the new life she'd wanted for so long.

"Do you remember those pictures we took on that high-school picnic, Ava?" Aunt Debbie said. "I was dating Rob back then, and you were with—"

"I remember," my mother said, cutting Aunt Debbie off. "We don't want to bore everyone with our old stories."

Well, there it was, the one thing that shifted my mother's normal control over her poker face – any mention of the past. Had my mother been at the picnic with one of my possible biological fathers? Was Aunt Debbie needling her, having had enough of the royal tour and my mom's keep-your-distance treatment? Or was Aunt Debbie merely innocently remembering a happy time? Only Mom and Aunt Debbie knew the answer to that.

"How about we show your family the rest of the house?" Greg said. All I wanted to do was sit down and gab. In fact what I was really wanted was to be sitting next to Adam at the Blue Jays baseball game he'd gone to, lucky dog. Being at the game with him would have made for a fun afternoon.

As we walked from room to room, Aunt Debbie's *oohing* and *aahing* was getting phonier and louder. Boy, was she ever laying it on thick. Grandy gave her a pinch, and my mother glared at her, but Greg didn't notice.

Throughout our royal tour, I could see Grandy and Aunt Debbie looking around to see if any of the pictures on mantles and dressers or walls were of our family. They kept glancing about until they gave up, Grandy becoming quiet, and Aunt Debbie sarcastic.

On the back wall of the den hung the few remaining family portraits of Greg, Janice, Jonathan, and Matt.

"Handsome boys," Grandy said.

Even Matt was annoyed by his father's exiling of their family pictures to the den. Jonathan was a lot more than annoyed. He was fuming. I had overheard him arguing with Greg about it, insisting their portraits should be in the living room and halls, along with the new ones. On this rare occasion, I completely sided with him.

"Let's see the upstairs Greg," my mother said, tapping Greg's arm.

Elspeth started to fuss. I patted her bottom to see if she was wet, but she wasn't. Probably she was as worn out by the tour as the rest of us. I jiggled her and then tickled her under the chin, but all my usual techniques failed.

Grandy reached to take her. As I was about to put Elspeth in her arms, Greg gave my mother a pointed look, telegraphing that he wanted her to take Elspeth. Mom hesitated, a torn, almost tortured expression on her face. She knew that whatever she did, she was going to end up hurting someone. This time, however, I wasn't going to let her off the hook. What was Greg's problem with Grandy holding her grandchild? What was wrong with that?

Greg was as overprotective and anxious as any new father, my mother would say constantly in his defence. Okay, I could kind of understand that. And okay, I could kind of get that he didn't think someone my age would know how to handle a baby. But Grandy? She'd raised two daughters and three grandchildren. My mom needed to start standing up to Greg when he needed to be stood up to, otherwise he was going to step all over her.

Finally, head down because she clearly couldn't face Grandy or Aunt Debbie, Mom intervened, taking Elspeth from me. She gazed at her and held her tightly, as if she were a shield.

Grandy looked as though she had been slapped in the face by Greg and worse, by Mom. Which she had been. I grabbed Grandy's hand and squeezed it and walked, leaning against her up the stairs. Aunt Debbie was quiet; she wasn't silent with hurt, as Grandy was. She was silent because she was too furious to speak – for now.

The last stop on the tour was my room. I pushed open the door and for the first time I saw a real smile on Grandy's face. I didn't bother looking at my mother's face. I knew how she'd look.

All over my room I had displayed pictures of my family. I'd printed out my very favorites from my computer and lined them up against my dresser mirror and against the wall behind my desk.

"I remember this fishing trip," Aunt Debbie said, going over to the print of Adam and me, dripping wet after our canoe had tipped. Fortunately Aunt Debbie and Chris had been fairly close to us in their canoe and had flipped ours over and rescued us and almost all of our fishing gear before it sank.

"Remember this?" I said, going over to the one of Grandy receiving her Employee of the Year award.

"Don't look so bad for an old lady, do I?" she said, smiling.

"Perm's too tight," Aunt Debbie teased. "No one to blame for that but me though, since I'm the one who gave it to you."

"If you hadn't yakked on the phone so long…" Grandy teased.

"*Ooh*, how about this one!" Aunt Debbie said. "You always did look terrific in that hostess outfit, Ava. Like a model."

My mom, who had been hurrying past the photos, eased her jogging pace.

Greg stepped closer to take a look, and then turned toward her with the kind of sappy, loving expression I wished Colin would have on his face while gazing at me. "Debbie's right," he said. "You look great!" Mom seemed delighted, yet still uncomfortable.

Greg sidled over to the photo of me, age seven, perched on

the edge of a buffet table, my mom standing next to me, holding a tray of refreshments. He smiled wider. "Phoebe's adorable in this picture! Look at those wide eyes and mischievous grin. You can certainly see that she and Elspeth are sisters."

I was pleased with the affection in Greg's voice – for me for once. I glanced over at Mom. "You kept that old photo all this time," she said, sounding surprised and starting to loosen up as Greg went over and embraced her.

"I like old photos," I said, more loudly and harshly than I had intended.

"Are these people relatives too?" Greg asked, pointing at the black-and-white pictures of Mrs. Tomblin and her family, then at the framed Malick print of the kids playing on the street.

In all the excitement of seeing Grandy and Aunt Debbie, I'd forgotten to check the back of the picture to see if it was one of the vintage prints. I would do that later, for sure.

I shook my head, trying to figure out what to say that wouldn't reveal the whoppers I had told about how I was spending my summer. "No, they belong to this elderly lady I've been helping out."

"Sweetness, these belong to Mrs. Tomblin, don't they?" Grandy asked.

I nodded. "We're visiting her tomorrow after lunch," Grandy announced.

"You never mentioned her to me," Mom said, now sounding not a bit hurt, but a lot hurt at being left out.

"I must have forgotten to tell you, Mom," I mumbled. What was I going to say? My social life this summer consisted of hanging out with an elderly lady who was losing her memory?

"Why do you have her family photographs?" Greg asked in a bemused voice. "Why wouldn't she keep them?"

The irony of that question was lost on Greg. He had exiled the photos of his first family to the hinterland of his den. My mom had no framed photos of her family at all; hers concealed in a storage bin in the basement.

Before I could come up with anything to say, Aunt Debbie chimed in. "Mrs. Tomblin gave the pictures to Phoebe for safe-keeping. She's moving into a retirement home, and there isn't much spare room for storing her things. Rather than having some family member bury the photos like toxic waste, she gave them to someone she knew would appreciate the comfort people receive from memories sparked by old photos."

chapter fourteen

"Yeah, yeah, yeah," Colin pretended to grumble. "Go ahead and toss the pictures of me and you onto the pile. See if I care. See if that doesn't break my heart." With that he flopped down onto the couch, his hands crossed over his heart.

"Faker, sit up!" I said, reaching over to grab his hands to yank him upright. He swatted me off.

Yesterday he'd brought his digital camera over to Mrs. Tomblin's to photograph the damage for the insurance company and the police. He'd also taken some pictures of her and me and had asked Mrs. Tomblin to take several pictures of him and me. He'd printed the photos and brought them along. I'd tossed them onto the pile of photos of the wrecked rooms because I didn't want him to catch me gazing googly-eyed at them.

"Hey," he said softly. Standing up, he put his hand gently on the back of my head.

"Hey," I said back, wanting to look away from his face. I was so nervous. He was going to kiss me. I leaned in and our lips touched. We kissed. Were getting ready to kiss again when the dratted doorbell rang. We looked at each other. I was breathing heavily. He didn't appear too calm either.

"I'll get the door," Colin said. "Maybe you should go wake up Mrs. Tomblin."

I went upstairs. Between the pain medications, her growing depression about leaving her house, and her Alzheimer's, Mrs. Tomblin was barely alert when she was awake. She was groggy, quiet, forgetful even early in the day, and all she wanted to do was sleep.

I heard voices downstairs, raised voices. One was Colin's, which was odd. I'd never heard him raise his voice. The other voice, a man's, was already at shout level.

"Mrs. Tomblin," I tapped her on the shoulder. "You have to wake up. There is somebody here to see you."

She looked up at me, bewildered, sleepy, out of it. I got her out of bed and helped her to dress. As we were leaving the bedroom, my arm wrapped around her waist, she paused for a moment, "Richard's here?" she asked.

Richard. I was going to finally meet Mr. Neglectful Son, and evidently in a bad mood. What joy! At least Colin and I were here to do what we could to keep him off his mother's back. This morning, at least.

"Richard's here," she repeated softly as we came down the stairs.

"Mother," he said, bending over her, his lips hovering like a fly above a kitchen table, never quite making it down to her cheek.

I knew what a real kiss was. And I might have enjoyed more than just one starter from Colin if Mr. Air Kisser hadn't started ringing the bell like a UPS delivery person trying to stay on schedule!

So this was Richard Tomblin, up close and personal. His brown hair was swept back from his forehead and it grazed the collar of his clearly expensive white shirt with French cuffs. Were those diamonds in his cuff links? Go on! He had on one of those pricey black pinstripe suits that Jonathan favored – only the best for the likes of Richard Tomblin and Dr. Jonathan Creighton. He was tall and well built, and yecch, on his fingernails, was that clear polish? Manicured nails? Give me a break.

"I'm Phoebe Hecht," I said, holding out my hand. When he shook it lightly – the handshake equivalent of the air kiss – I saw that I was correct. His nails *were* manicured and those cufflinks had diamonds in them, as did his Rolex watch. "My friend Colin Flanagan and I have been helping your mother clean up after the robbery and with making a list of the damaged and stolen items."

Richard stared at Colin. "I knew I recognized you. The stock boy from Max's Marketplace."

His tone was so patronizing, I flinched for Colin.

"That is so good of you," he said. "My mother is fortunate to have helpers."

Friends, you jerk, not helpers. I was seething, but attempted a smile all the same. "How was your vacation?" I asked. "*You enjoyed yourself?*" *In other words, you selfish creep, your mother was in intensive care and you were working on your tan on some beach in Capri.*

Mrs. Tomblin gazed at him impassively. She must have given

up long ago on getting any real caring from the tanned creep. She didn't seem hurt or disappointed that Richard hadn't cut his vacation short. I thought she was being stoical. Likely, though, it was simply resignation.

Apparently she was on to Richard, and had been for ages. As sad as that was, maybe it was better. Why have expectations of Mr. Neglectful Son when she would only be let down?

"Mother, let me help you over to the couch," he said. "Didn't it used to be adjacent to the front window?" He looked around the living room as if unfamiliar with the changes.

"I moved the couch away from the window a while back," she replied. "The draft from the window was chilling me in the winter."

Richard sat down next to her on the couch. "You don't look too bad. That's encouraging!"

He must be looking at her with his eyes shut. She looked terrible. Was he saying that to make her feel better, or to make himself feel better for not cutting his vacation short? I'd place my bet on the latter.

"How was your trip?" she asked politely, as though he hadn't said a word to her about appearance. While he ran through his itinerary, I went to the kitchen and brought out some cold drinks, fruits and cookies on a tray. I sat down on the arm of the wing chair, where Colin was sitting.

"Thank you, Phoebe," Mrs. Tomblin said gratefully.

"Yes, thanks," Richard said perfunctorily.

There were papers and forms spread out on top of the photos Colin had taken. I twisted around to see what they were. Insurance forms.

"It is necessary that you sign these, Mother," Richard said, the exasperation in his voice announcing that he was about to lose what miniscule amount of patience he had with his mother.

"When I have read them over, I will sign them," she said.

I shrugged at Colin. It had been my experience, and Colin's as well, that Mrs. Tomblin was way too passive and went along with whoever was willing to make a decision for her. Not this time though. The Richard effect. He was so piggy and controlling he brought out the resistance reserves. If he said black, you wanted to say white.

Or maybe it was that Mrs. Tomblin had years and years of practice resisting Richard's "help." Like his "help" selling her long-time home and storing her and what little remained of the possessions she loved in an old age home.

"Mother, the claims payment will get delayed," he whined.

"I'm not spending much money these days," she said. "No rush for me."

Was she needling him?

"Mother, Mother," he said shaking his head and looking over at us. "There are many valuables in the house requiring replacement and reimbursement. In the meantime, that insurance money could be invested, and you could be collecting interest."

Considering the couch move was a big surprise to him, it was obvious he hardly ever visited his mother. And when he did, he probably never made it out of the living and dining room area. So would he know what valuable items were or weren't in the house?

"I want to read the forms," she said stubbornly.

Richard sighed and looked over at Colin and me, presuming

we would be supportive. *Try again in an alternate universe. Try when hell freezes over!*

"My mother gets so easily confused these days," he said to us, as if his mother wasn't sitting beside him and hearing every word. "You understand why these forms have to be signed, don't you?"

The phone rang. The only working phone in the house was the wall phone in the kitchen and I hurried to answer it, glad for the interruption.

I wasn't so glad when I answered. It was Constable Murdoch. Jeez, the place was raining creeps today. One sat on the couch, fiddling with his cufflinks and peeking at his Rolex. I guess he'd already put in more minutes than he'd planned. The other was mouth-breathing into my ear.

"Who is it, Phoebe?" Mrs. Tomblin asked.

"Constable Murdoch."

Richard stopped fiddling with his cufflinks. I assumed – as most people would have – that he would handle the call. I pointed at the phone, gesturing for him to come over and speak to the constable. He shook his head no.

Bizarre. Not much time to contemplate the bizarreness with Constable Murdoch barking questions into my ear as if I were some suspect he was interrogating.

"Got the list of stolen items yet?"

"Not yet."

"She remember anything about the burglary, her attackers?"

"Not yet."

He then recited a list of questions as though he was reading from a police manual checklist. My answers to the questions were no, maybe, not yet, no, no, and not yet.

While I was answering, I watched Mrs. Tomblin chat with Colin who was trying to distract her with a funny story. However, it was like Richard was the one really in need of distraction. He was an advertisement for nervous ticks, adjusting his cufflinks, combing his hair back with his fingers, and jiggling his legs.

The longer I remained on the phone, the antsier he got. Did he think I wasn't handling it efficiently? Why didn't he take over then? You'd think he'd be satisfied that the police were on the job. Wouldn't police involvement speed up the payment of the insurance claims? After all, that was the reason he was here.

"Yes, I'll call you as soon as she remembers," I said, hanging up the phone and heading toward the living room to resume the battle over the claims forms. Suddenly, Richard stood up to go. Hallelujah!

"Mother, I would appreciate it if you could read the forms and sign them promptly," he said, straining to be polite. "And I would *greatly* appreciate your assistance," he added, facing Colin and me. "Give me a call when my mother signs the forms, and I will send a courier to pick them up."

He handed me his business card. Richard M. Tomblin, Investment Analyst, Sterling, White and Thurman Investments.

"Speak to you soon," he said to his mother, his parting words sounding like a warning.

Colin and I followed him to the door. He paused and took two fifties out of his wallet. "Please take this…in gratitude," he said.

Colin flushed, unmistakably angry and insulted. "Mr. Tomblin, Phoebe and I like your mother. We want to help her.

Please," he said, holding up his hand like a stop signal, "your gratitude is noted."

That was diplomacy at work. I would have told him to stuff his money.

"Phoebe has your card," he said. "She will call you when your mother has completed the forms."

Neither of Colin's answers were the ones Richard had expected. But what could he do? If we hadn't been there, he might have forced her to sign. And what scared me was that I could imagine him doing it literally...and not just with words.

chapter fifteen

I was going through the insurance inventory with Mrs. Tomblin, marking the items that had been either damaged or stolen.

"That's not missing?" she asked, pointing to the first item on the list, the sterling silver cutlery set. She looked at me with that bewildered look I knew too well – as though she didn't trust her memory. How awful, I thought, to have to live like that, always unsure whether you were remembering or forgetting.

She had remembered, though. The cutlery set wasn't missing; it was in the top drawer of the dining room buffet. We had shown it to the constable, hadn't we? To be certain I went to the drawer and opened it. The set was there.

"Those aren't missing either," Mrs. Tomblin said, trying, I could tell, to sound positive. The next things listed were her jewelry – the diamond wedding ring, the matching diamond band, the cultured pearls, the diamond pendant and the Cartier watch. They were in the dresser drawer in Mrs. Tomblin's bedroom. Still,

I went upstairs to double-check. All there.

Downstairs, back in the living room, we returned to the list. Jeez, she must have been paying a mint for this policy because the value of the items seemed highballed to me. I knew nothing about insurance policies, but it did seem a waste of money to insure possessions that could be replaced more cheaply than paying such pricey premiums.

The ancient TV had been valued at a thousand dollars. It never could have been worth that much. It was gone, so I checked it off. Her even more ancient VCR was valued at four hundred dollars. Was I missing something here? It was gone too, so I checked it off, along with her three-hundred-dollar portable phone and the priciest appliances outside of a designer kitchen.

Then we went through the figurines which had been smashed, and the lamps, and the slashed couch. I marked damage beside each of them.

This all took much longer than I thought it would. I hadn't even gotten upstairs or to the photographs by the time Colin arrived with our dinner – salmon steaks, vegetable soup, pasta salad, and a carrot cake – courtesy of Max's excellent takeout. As I warmed up the dinner on the stove, I heard Colin on the phone.

"Da, I'm at Mrs. Tomblin's now. I'll be home before nine-thirty. Yeah, yeah, I didn't buy a pizza. I got the salmon, yeah, yeah, tell Ma, just like she ordered." He laughed. "Change that to recommended."

"Oh great," I muttered to myself. I had forgotten to call Mom and Greg to tell them that I wouldn't be there for dinner. Not that I was there, really, even when I was there. I had hardly spoken to my mother since Grandy, Aunt Debbie, and Adam had returned home.

Her pretence that everything was all right, all settled between us, was hard enough to take. But then we spoke to Grandy on the phone this morning, and I could hear (and, of course, so could Mom) the distress and reserve in her voice. Yet Mom continued with her "everything was all right" pretence with Grandy, too.

All the grievances that I'd been bottling up for months had flooded out after that call. I couldn't take one second more of the sham.

"How come you never tell Greg to cool it when I play with Elspeth, that I know how to take care of a baby? Didn't I take care of the neighbors' babies and kids? They trusted me, didn't they? They kept on hiring me didn't they?"

"You have to understand that Greg is overprotective of Elspeth," she replied. "Elspeth is the first girl he's had, and he's like any new father, anxious and watchful," my mom said, trembling as I glowered at her.

"How come understanding applies to everyone except Greg and you, huh?" I yelled. "I've heard those same old excuses from you since Elspeth was born. He's not a new dad, okay? And besides, he should know I would never, ever, do anything to hurt Elspeth."

"Of course, we both know that. Fears and anxieties aren't rational sometimes," she said.

"Well you should know *that* better than anyone, shouldn't you? You don't let any of us say a single word about our life in Barrie, as if everybody and everything from our past shames you. It made you *uncomfortable* to have our family pictures out, so I stowed them away. And when I finally bucked you and put them back out, you were embarrassed by them in front of Greg, even though you saw how interested he was in them. Didn't you meet Greg in your horribly embarrassing past? Doesn't he know mostly all about it? Isn't he proud of you and what you accomplished? Didn't he ask you to marry him, knowing all that?"

I was heaving by then and had to stop to catch my breath. My mom was just standing there, stunned. Then after a long stare-down between us, she opened her mouth to speak. But before she could say anything, I exploded, finally saying out loud what wounded the most. "You make me feel like you're ashamed that you ever had me!"

"No! Never, never!" my mom cried. "How can you say that? I love you so much and am so proud of you. Proud of us."

"Then show it! To Greg. To his friends!"

"You need to understand, Phoebe, I worry. Compared to Greg's friends and their wives, I *am* uneducated, and you have seen how some of them have behaved..." she whispered.

"I *do* understand, Mom. You know I do. So does Grandy. So does Aunt Debbie. We have *understood* for too long. Don't *you* understand that you have been treating us the same way Greg's friends have been treating you?" She swiped at her tears. Was she tearing up because of regret or because she was feeling sorry for herself?

"Phoebe, I love Greg. This is our fairytale come true," she said softly.

"*Yours*, not ours. Your fairytale is becoming our family nightmare!"

We both stood silent, me because I was hoarse and wiped, she maybe because what I had said was sinking in.

In a choked whisper, she said, "I understand. I do. And I'm sorry. Things will change. You'll see. I promise."

That was what I had wanted her to say for months. And if I had heard it before the weekend with Grandy, I would have been choked up myself, and I would have hugged my mom. But I couldn't forget how Grandy, who seldom cried, had burst into tears later that evening in the restaurant she and Aunt Debbie had taken Adam and me to after the baseball game. The rest of the weekend Grandy had been reserved with my mom, Aunt Debbie fuming mad, and Adam sullen.

"You going to say that to Grandy, Aunt Debbie, Chris, and Adam? You owe them a big apology! And *saying* sorry isn't enough. It takes *doing* things differently."

Before she could say anything more, I raced out of the house.

"You didn't remember to tell your parents?" Colin asked, his hand on my forearm, smiling at me as if it was an innocent mistake. Not a mistake. "I'll get out of your way, and you can call."

"No, no," I said. "I have my BlackBerry." Walking away from Colin and toward the living room, I took it out of my pocket, hoping that Greg was home and would answer. He did, and I mechanically told him my standard lie. Having dinner with Yuri at her house. I would be home after nine. Yuri would be thrilled to find just how many wonderful dinners I'd enjoyed at her house this summer – considering she lived in a school dormitory and her parents' house was in a Tokyo suburb.

"Can I do something?" Mrs. Tomblin asked as I came back

into the kitchen. I was about to say you don't have to bother, but Colin jumped in.

"Could you put on a pot of tea? And would you slice up the carrot cake? A thick slice for me. I'm a growing boy, remember?" he teased.

She smiled as she got up. "I remember. You like the lemon zinger herbal tea best."

"That I do, Mrs. Tomblin."

"Two teaspoons of brown sugar?"

He nodded.

She hobbled slowly to the stove and put on the kettle, humming to herself. She needed to feel useful, and being included and being asked to do something, made her feel good about herself. I needed to start doing that too, instead of just doing everything for her because (the noble reason) I wanted to help and because (the not-so-noble reason) I could do it quicker.

It was early evening and I started to worry that Mrs. Tomblin was going to get dozy and forgetful before we got to the inventory of the photographs, but this was a good evening for her. After we had gobbled up the carrot cake, we went into the living room to finish off the list.

Rachel Malick's photographs were on the last page, saving the best and most valuable for last. Colin whistled, as surprised as I was by how high they'd been assessed, and he knew a lot about Malick's work.

The assessments ranged from forty thousand to ninety-five thousand dollars. The ninety-five-thousand-dollar photograph was a platinum print; the rest were vintage silver gelatin prints.

"Five of the six that were hanging there are missing," I said, pointing to the wall. "I have one. Mrs. Tomblin gave it to me. I had no idea at the time that it might be valuable."

"Did you check the back?" Colin asked.

I nodded. Finally I had. "They're all titled and numbered," I said, looking at the list on the insurance form. "Whoa! I have the platinum print!"

"That's the one of kids playing on the street," Colin said, excitedly.

"One of my favorites," Mrs. Tomblin said.

"It's one of Rachel Malick's most famous pictures," Colin added.

We all were silent for a moment. I was relieved that it, at least, hadn't been stolen.

"What do we do to keep it safe…if you're right, Colin?" I asked.

Now that I had learned just what those photographs were worth, Colin's theory seemed the most likely one. The thieves had targeted Mrs. Tomblin's and were after the photographs. This was one case where you hoped they were, because then they would be selling them off. But if they had grabbed them just because they were there, they might already be destroyed and in some garbage dump.

Then it hit Colin. "Whoever wanted those photographs knew there were ten vintage prints," he said suddenly.

"How would they know that?" I asked

"Remember the newspaper article? It said that Mrs. Tomblin had kept ten of her favorite vintage photographs and a number of reprints and had bequeathed the vintage prints to the Art Gallery of Ontario in her will."

Of course, Mrs. Tomblin hadn't known then that she was about to be shipped off to a retirement home where she'd be lucky if she had the wall space to hang up even one or two.

"I want them back! They're mine!" Mrs. Tomblin said, hugging herself. "I promised Aunt Rachel that I would take good care of them, and they're gone! I shouldn't have kept them. I should have given them all to the Art Gallery." She started to weep, and I wrapped my arm around her and patted her shoulder. I wasn't a crier. It took a lot to get me to cry. Now though, I was this close to crying myself, I felt so bad for her.

"Mrs. Tomblin," Colin said. He was kneeling in front of her. "I know it pains you to think you may have lost the photographs forever. Phoebe has one, and the other four vintage prints may still be here in the house. Do you remember where you hung them?"

I hoped like anything that Colin was right. That somehow those other four hadn't been snatched. I had never seen them and I had been in the house many times.

Mrs. Tomblin took a deep breath. I watched her work to remember. "My husband's study. Upstairs."

Colin took one arm and I the other, and we went upstairs. I'd never been in the study. It was next to Mrs. Tomblin's bedroom, and the door was always closed. She turned the knob and we went in. There were four photographs over a leather couch, three over a desk, and five more on either side of the window.

"They're here!" She went to stare at the pictures over the desk.

"The vintage prints, I think, are the ones hanging over the couch," Colin whispered. "You can tell by the rich tones and the paper. Look at the ones over the desk. You can see the difference."

I nodded, and he took them off the wall, one by one, checking to see if they were numbered and signed. They were. He sighed with relief and turned to Mrs. Tomblin.

"I have a suggestion, Mrs. Tomblin," Colin said. "Do you think it might be a good idea to donate these four to the gallery now, and the one Phoebe has, too?"

"Yes, I must," she said softly, moving to Colin's side. She stared at the photos and then turned around slowly as if she had to force herself to stop looking at them.

"Do you have the name of the curator?" he asked. We both saw from her anxious look that she didn't remember the name.

"I have a program from the exhibition. The curator's name is on it, and I will call and ask her to have the photos picked up. They know about the robbery so they will come right away. That will keep the photos safe and sound."

"Thank you Colin. You're such a good boy. And Phoebe, you're priceless. I can't thank you enough," Mrs. Tomblin said quietly. "I think I will go to bed. I'm so very tired."

"I'll clean up the kitchen and lock up," I told her as she left the room.

Colin took my hand and at his touch, I got tingly. "You're priceless, Phoebe," Colin said.

I thought for a moment he was razzing me, and he was a bit, but then he bent over and kissed me again. Now *that* was priceless.

chapter sixteen

Lying in bed, scheming instead of sleeping, I came up with what I considered to be a most excellent setup to identify the burglars. Finally, finally, reading all those Agatha Christie mysteries – combined with Yuri's instruction in detecting – was paying off.

While walking me home, Colin had told me that stolen art was a tremendous moneymaker for criminals, right up there with drug dealing and selling guns. Six billion dollars worth of art was stolen yearly. The ten Malick photographs were valued at over half a million dollars, according to the insurance assessments. This was one instance when the assessed value on the policy was lower than what the vintage prints would go for in an art auction.

So assuming – didn't all detectives, amateur or not, assume? – the target had been the photos, the burglars must figure there are five more that they hadn't found. I was too buzzed to fall asleep. With the time difference, Yuri should be waking up soon in Tokyo. I went to my computer and e-mailed her.

Dear Miss Kimura, the Tokyo but soon-to-be once again the premier Toronto Miss Marple,
Just as you detected, you brainiac, it seems pretty likely (how's that for sounding certain) that Mrs. Tomblin's house was targeted. The crooks were after Rachel Malick's photographs. Who knew photographs could be worth that much? You, probably, and Colin too. You know how in crime shows, the police always attend the funerals of murder victims to see if the murderer shows up for the service, and they photograph all the mourners and check them out. Does this really happen? It beats me. If I murdered someone, I sure as heck wouldn't be showing up at the funeral. Why? I murdered the person. I know he or she is dead. Am I showing up to admire my handiwork? Am I showing up to taunt the police? This is beyond me. Anyway, it gave me a crazy idea of how to possibly finger the suspects. There's confidence for you, but I'm not in the brainiac league, What would you think if I got Mrs. Tomblin to hold another garage sale? The garage sale could kind of act like a funeral does for a murder victim – draw the burglars to come to check out whether the photos are still in the house. Naturally, they aren't going to be. Mrs. Tomblin has already donated them to gallery.

I could get Colin to take pictures on the sly of who showed up...and then take the pictures to the police.

Just hit me like a rock slide. How about just hit me
with a rock? This would put Mrs. Tomblin in danger,
wouldn't it? The burglars beat her up last time. And
the constable assigned to the case...why would he
even waste his time looking at a bunch of photos
taken by kids? Plus, if the Malick photographs are
at the gallery, what is there to trap the burglars
with? Scratch this. What a super dunce, huh!

Phoebe, who is unworthy of being called the
Toronto Miss Marple

I slumped in the chair, now feeling dense and guilt ridden,
instead of buzzed. Great friend I was to Mrs. Tomblin, making
her a target. There must be a way to both protect Mrs. Tomblin
and lure in the burglars. How though? I heard a message ping.
Yuri had already answered.

Dear Miss Hecht,
the most worthy to be called the Toronto Miss Marple,
You must be watching the same crime shows I watch (I
already know you are reading the same mysteries I am
because I'm making you). It is a good idea. You might even
recognize the burglars yourself. I bet they *were* at the first
garage sale.

You're right though. It could put Mrs. Tomblin in danger if
she stays in the house after the sale. Isn't she going to a
retirement home soon?

And...I just have to know. It's Colin this and Colin that. You and Colin? Are you and Colin a you and Colin? Do tell, do tell, do tell. You better tell me or else....

Yuri

I had to pause here. Were Colin and I an *us*? Did two kisses make us an us? As much as I wanted to think so, that sappy I wasn't. We were kind of an us...*becoming* an us. Stop it. It wasn't like I had tons of experience being an us. What to say?

Yuri,
Colin and I, we've become good friends. I liked him a lot before, and I like him a lot more now. You can see for yourself when you get back and tell me what you think about that, too.

Now back to Mrs. Tomblin. How about this? It just came to me. Okay, she would have to go for this. We have the garage sale. Then she leaves the house for good. She can stay with...Matt! His roommate is on vacation, and Mrs. Tomblin can sleep in his bedroom. I can stay there too, until she goes to the retirement home. Of course, Mrs. Tomblin has to agree, Matt has to agree, and maybe this is just all ridiculous...I don't know anymore.

Phoebe

Phoebe,
There are a lot of big ifs here. Run it by Colin. He won't do anything dumb or dangerous. Not like us detective wan-nabes, living in Miss Marple land. Bonus, more quality time with Colin. I detect you're not telling all. I'll get it out of you in person. I have my Miss Marple ways! I'd sign off with don't do anything I wouldn't do, but that's not good advice. Instead, I'll sign off with don't do anything Colin wouldn't do. My cell is on 24/7. Text me night and day.

Yuri

Yuri was right on about Colin. He wouldn't do anything dumb or dangerous. I shut off my computer. Now if I could just manage to move from scheming to sleeping before morning.

chapter seventeen

Jeez, the next time one of the guidance counselors asked me what profession I was interested in pursuing, rather than my stock "I haven't decided yet," finally I had an answer – garage sale manager. This was the third sale I'd organized for Mrs. Tomblin. Her neighbors were greeting me as though they knew me when they saw me, which they did by this time. Their bargaining was friendly. None of the unfriendly bargainers had shown up yet; the types that weren't satisfied unless they bought something at such a low price that they might as well have stolen it.

I glanced over at the living room windows. The drapes had been opened, pushed to the side, yet I couldn't glimpse Colin and his camera. He was well hidden behind the drapes.

As Yuri had predicted, Colin had proved to be Mr. Common Sense and Mr. Careful. After my brainstorming e-mails with Yuri, I'd made arrangements to meet him at Mrs. Tomblin's to outline my scheme. I was anxious for two reasons.

Reason one: I didn't want to do anything that would put Mrs. Tomblin in danger – nor Colin or me.

Reason two: I didn't want Colin and Mrs. Tomblin to think I was an impulsive daredevil who'd been reading too many mysteries and watching too many TV crime shows.

At first, Colin had said finding out who did it was not worth the risk of putting Mrs. Tomblin in any possible danger. He realized, as did I, that the burglars had not expected Mrs. Tomblin to be home or that she would fight to protect the photographs. But they had fought too.

Colin also told me that only ten percent of stolen art was ever recovered and the criminals caught. Therefore, the odds weren't good that we would be able to find out who did it, and even if by some miracle we did, getting the photographs returned to Mrs. Tomblin was not very probable.

Mrs. Tomblin, however, had said yes to my scheme. Yes, yes, yes, so relentlessly that it had been almost scary. She felt so guilty about letting her aunt down. She could be awfully stubborn, and I could imagine what she'd been like when she was younger. I bet she'd been a fireball, just like Grandy.

I'd asked Matt if Mrs. Tomblin could stay with him, and he'd said yes, of course. The adventure intrigued him, as did the fact that Mrs. Tomblin was the niece of Rachel Malick. Turns out he'd visited the Malick exhibition, having admired her work for years. Mrs. Tomblin would go to Matt's immediately after the garage sale. No problem either, with my sleeping over at Matt's. My mother had looked as relieved as I was to have a break from the awkward, agonizing politeness that passed for conversation between us.

Colin had an idea, a terrific one, on how to attract the burglars. Malick's photographs were safe. The curator had picked them up along with the platinum print Mrs. Tomblin had given me. We knew that, but the burglars didn't.

To make them believe Mrs. Tomblin still had the prints in her possession, Colin had brought over his two framed Malick reproductions and hung them over the living room couch. If the suspects neared the porch and looked in the living room window, the reproductions would look real enough to pass.

All three of us, Colin in the living room, Mrs. Tomblin in a lawn chair in the shade of the garage, and I, wandering around, were in wait-and-see mode. Truth be told, Mrs. Tomblin had run out of things that anyone would want – even for free. What little we had for sale came from Colin and his family, Matt, and me. I had no old stuff; the garage sales back in Barrie had cleaned me out. I brought some new and hardly worn clothing. Colin had brought used clothing from his parents and sisters, kitchen gadgets, cookware, and books. The best items had come from Matt: CDs, audio books, paperbacks and hardcovers, DVDs, clothing, magazines, and movie posters.

Even so, it was a pretty mingy garage sale. The few people looking around were hardly even picking anything up. No surprise, the first set of Matt's items that I put out went fast. Actually, those were the only things that went. Sales were so slow I had plenty of time to wander about and make it back over the garage whenever somebody was ready to pay.

Most of the people were neighbors, middle-aged and older couples, who didn't seem like the sort that would break into Mrs. Tomblin's house and beat her up. Mrs. Tomblin was telling anyone who came near her all about Rachel Malick's photography, the whole story about the robbery and the photographs that remained. As she got tired out, she started repeating her stories, especially this one about going with her aunt on a photo shoot.

Rachel Malick had no clear idea of what she was going to photograph when she strolled downtown carrying her 35 mm miniature Leica. What was it Colin had told us about the camera? It was as famous as the photographers who had used it, like Walker Evans and Henri Cartier-Bresson. It was compact, lightweight, silent, and had a rapid shutter speed, which made it a favorite of street photographers like Rachel Malick who liked to work quickly and capture people before they were aware of the lens.

The niece Malick adored had frequently accompanied her aunt on these outings. Malick had called them "picture-taking safaris." Since she didn't want people to realize she was photographing them, she used a wide viewfinder so it would seem she was never pointing her camera directly at them.

The story Mrs. Tomblin was relating was about how her aunt had shot another of my favorite photographs. She said that her aunt was standing on one side of the street, leaning against a building and heard a couple arguing on the other side of the street. She glanced over, then sighted a man dancing across the street, and started snapping pictures. Mrs. Tomblin remembered what her aunt said, what her aunt wore, what she wore, what the weather was like, where they went afterward for lunch, and what they ate – grilled cheese sandwiches, French fries with gravy, and cherry colas.

Fascinating story, the first time I had heard it, but by the tenth telling, I could have recited it word for word along with Mrs. Tomblin. At least there were new people coming by to hear it. Were any of them burglars?

I went over to check on her. These days, the combination of stress, guilt, and fear was making her clear-headed moments fairly short-lived.

"Hey, are you okay out here?" I asked, crouching beside her.

"Could be better," she said sighing, and then added, "could be worse."

I rose and squeezed her shoulder, not knowing what to say. Everything was packed away. The suitcases were at the retirement home, waiting for her arrival (incarceration was more like it, at least that was my view), and I'd stored the overnight case she was taking to Matt's in the front closet. This was her last afternoon in her home.

"I'll bring you some lemonade and fruit," I said. She nodded wearily.

I went inside. Colin was resting against the wall, his eyes shutting and opening wide as though he were fighting to stay awake. "No mugs to take mug shots of, huh?" I said, going over to him.

"Only your mug!" he teased, aiming his camera at me and taking a shot.

"That's too close up!" I laughed. "You want to capture my blackheads, go ahead." I touched his arm. "Want some lemonade? I'm getting a glass for Mrs. Tomblin."

"How's she keeping?" He peered out the window. "She looks worn out from here."

"She is. Heat and everything else," I said. "Maybe the lemonade and a fruit salad will perk her up." I peeked out the window. "There are some fresh mugs coming up the driveway for you to shoot!"

"So there are!" he said, and went back to taking pictures with his zoom lens.

More of a crowd had gathered by the time I got back with the drinks and fruit. More buyers or more suspects? Hard to tell. Everyone was starting to look like a suspect to me.

Was it the city worker heading toward Mrs. Tomblin's backyard to read the electrical meter? He would be familiar enough with the back of the house to know where to break in, plus he'd probably carry tools that could be used for a break in. He could have used those to pick the lock.

When he was finished, he circled the tables, picked up four T-shirts, formerly mine, and came over to pay for them. "Got three daughters," he said, wiping the sweat off his face with his sleeve. "The youngest is about your size, and she constantly complains, can't blame her, about having to wear her sister's hand-me-downs. These seem nearly new. In style, huh?"

I crossed him off my list. Some nice dad did not seem the type to punch Mrs. Tomblin and steal from her. Then I sighted two grungy girls with spiky black hair dyed and more piercings in their eyebrows than eyebrow hair. They were carrying hobo purses, better to steal with, I figured, so I followed their every move like a store security guard. The taller of the two slipped a DVD into her purse, then another two. I leapt up and ran over.

"I saw that," I said. "Hand them over!"

"You gonna make me, little girl?" she hooted, shoving me.

I shoved her back. She fell down and I grabbed her bag and took out the DVDs. "I guess I did," I said, standing there with my hands resting on hips, hoping I looked tough. I felt tough. She got up, noticed people staring, then signaled to her friend and headed down the driveway. What do you know? I had nabbbed a suspect. Maybe it was a sign.

I went back to sizing up people and suspecting them for a minute, then crossing them off my list when they bought something and were friendly. Some real suspects had better show up soon. Mrs. Tomblin had fallen asleep, and her snoring, along with the heat, was making me sleepy too.

I jerked in my lawn chair when the sound of a booming muffler polluted the air and airwaves. Three guys got out of a new purple Mustang, a cruddy imitation of an old-style Mustang, which was a cool car. Aunt Debbie used to drive one – not a restored vintage in her case, but a used car.

One of them stood smoking, leaning against the car, while the other two swaggered across the street over to the tables closest to the curb. Those displayed the cheapest and least likely to be sold or stolen stuff – an old toaster and four-cup coffeemaker, mismatched cups and saucers, and a desk lamp.

One guy, wearing a puke green T-shirt, mauled the books and the cups, then yelled out, "Quick, toss me the hand-sanitizer, will ya Gary!" Gary thought this was hilarious and bent over the table, killing himself laughing.

I straightened up in the chair. These two were the hosers who had tossed the figurines at the first garage sale. The guy in green looked over at me, gave me a smile, then winked, just as he had the last time – his standard move with any female of any age, I supposed.

As the Winker and Gary swaggered up the driveway with as much hip movement as Elvis Presley, I glanced over at the front window and saw the tip of Colin's zoom lens. If nothing else, their mug shots would be good for a laugh.

They swiveled over to the table with Matt's stuff on it. The Winker snatched up some DVDs and a Hawaiian shirt, and Gary, who didn't look like the tie-wearing type, grabbed two. Then I remembered the cartoon characters on those ties – Homer Simpson and Mickey Mouse. The tie made the man. Was that how the saying sort of went? Oh so true, in this case.

"Hello ladies, remember us? We've been here before," the Winker said, winking.

Mrs. Tomblin woke up with a jerk and looked at them with a perplexed expression. She was at her worst after waking; it took her a while to become alert.

"*I* remember you, is that good enough?" I said, and from the way I said it, even he clued in. "Those DVDs are a dollar apiece and the shirt is three. Seven bucks."

"I can count," he said, not winking and not sounding like a pick-up artist anymore.

"That's good, it's a useful skill to have," I said. He practically threw his money at me.

"Mrs. Tomblin, it's me, Gary, your old paperboy," Gary said, and laughed like he had said something funny. A moron and high, what a loser!

"The paperboy who was always tossing the paper into the

lilac bush, rather than onto the porch," Mrs. Tomblin said. He must have done that often for her to still remember.

This time I laughed. "Some pitcher's arm you got there, Gary! You think you can toss over the two bucks you owe for the ties? I'm a good catcher." He threw the money at me. I gave him a wink.

They both stood there, scowling at me. "Thank you for your purchases," I said, getting nervous. Maybe I shouldn't have been so mouthy because now they didn't look like goofs, they looked mean – scary mean.

The Winker bent close to Mrs. Tomblin. "How'd you get this stuff? It's not yours." How would he know that? Okay, it was obvious that Mrs. Tomblin wouldn't have had any Homer Simpson and Mickey Mouse ties lying around. Still, she could have had a DVD player.

Yet he had said "It's not yours" as if he knew for sure. Were they really suspect material, or did I just want them to be?

chapter eighteen

I was giving myself a pep talk as I sat on a bench across from the Information desk at the police station. It was hard to sit when I was so wired. I would have liked to join the two men and one women pacing the small area as they waited to speak to a constable about…well, no one came to a police precinct to speak about anything good.

"How long have you been here?" I asked the woman as she passed me.

"Too long!" she said. "Forty-seven minutes too long."

I was curious about why she was here, hoping that she might take a break from her pacing. I was the newbie in the waiting area, having arrived only twenty minutes earlier to hand over the photos Colin took at the garage sale.

She continued pacing, though, and I returned to giving myself a pep talk. *You go girl. Do not let Constable Murdoch get to you. You are not going to talk back or get defensive and sarcastic. The goal here is to get Constable Murdoch to take the pictures seriously, remember?*

I was on the third go-round of my pep talk when the constable at the Information desk called me over. The woman pacing had gone inside five minutes ago and the men soon after that. "The squad meeting Constable Murdoch is in should conclude any minute," she said. "I'll buzz him ASAP and let him know that you need to see him."

"Thanks, I appreciate it," I said. "I only want want to give him these photos."

"No worries," she said, with a smile. A friendly constable, what a pleasant change! Instead of returning to my chair I stood there, and to pass the time – hers and mine – we chatted. She was the Community Relations Officer, and I asked her what her job was like.

"Like a 911 operator, advice counselor and concierge, all rolled into one hectic package," she said, with a grin. "Frantically busy followed by excruciating lulls with nothing doing. I prefer it frantic. It makes the day interesting."

She buzzed Constable Murdoch again. "Oh, Constable Murdoch got called out to an investigation," she said.

"When should I come back?" I asked, determined to give him the photos, even if it took coming several times a day until I could hand them over.

"No need to come back," she said. "Let me see if you can talk to Constable Murdoch's new partner." She made another call, and made arrangements for me to meet with Constable Patchett in the cafeteria.

There were police officers at all the cafeteria tables. How the heck was I supposed to find Constable Patchett? Great detective I was, I'd forgotten to ask what Constable Murdoch's partner looked like.

Suddenly a blond woman stood up and waved me over. When I reached the table, she pulled out a chair for me and shook my hand. "I'm Constable Christine Patchett," she said. "Pleased to meet you." Definitely not a clone of Constable Murdoch.

"I'm Phoebe Hecht," I said, beaming as though I'd won the lottery. "Pleased to meet you too." How pleased she would never guess, though maybe I was wrong about that. Constable Murdoch was her partner, after all, so everyone who met her after dealing with Murdoch was probably as gaga with relief as I was.

She was about my height, in her mid-twenties, and from her muscular build, she looked as if she was into sports as much as I was. Another bonus point.

"Constable Rutherford filled me in. You have some information that could prove useful in the Tomblin burglary?"

I quickly recited my memorized summary about the last garage sale. She nodded as she listened, then asked pointed questions, clearly interested, and clearly not considering me someone suffering from Nancy Drew delusions.

"I went to the exhibition of Malick's photographs. They are remarkable!"

I must have looked startled because Constable Patchett smiled at me. "Don't I look like the artsy type to you?"

"I didn't even know photographs could be so valuable and hang in galleries before I met Mrs. Tomblin," I mumbled.

"Me either," she said. "Not until I was assigned to the

Property and Evidence Management Unit. I had to do a crash course in art, antique history, and jewelry appraisal. I got hooked, and now I'm a regular art and museum goer. Keep my secret a secret around here, will you?" she kidded.

"Will do," I said, and smiled.

"Let's get down to business," she said.

As I spread the photos out on the table, the copy I'd made of the insurance inventory fluttered out, and I handed it to the constable. She read it carefully, and as she did, it hit me – given how valuable the photographs were, why hadn't Richard, once he was at his mother's house and saw that some were missing, checked to see if the rest were there? Why hadn't Mr. Moneybags ever reported that the prints had been stolen?

Should I mention that to Constable Patchett? I decided to keep my suspicions to myself for now and pass them by Yuri and Colin later.

I watched Constable Patchett examine the photographs, and then she picked one up. "You know this guy?" she asked. It was the photo of a man leaning against the Mustang smoking.

"No, I never saw him before, but I have seen the two guys he came with," I pointed to a picture of the two hosers beside a table.

Constable Patchett held both photos up and stared at them. "Thank you very much, and please thank your friend Colin for me."

"You're welcome," I said and didn't add what I was thinking. *Thanks for not treating me like a know-nothing kid, getting in the way of solving the case.* Unlike her partner, Constable Patchett managed to be both professional and a people person.

I got up to leave and the constable stood up as well. "We can take it from here, okay?" she said, sounding concerned.

I nodded. What else could I do? Even though I felt her concern was genuine and not a brush-off, the case wasn't over until it was really over. Until then, for all sorts of reasons, first among them, helping Mrs. Tomblin keep her promise to her aunt, I wasn't about to butt out.

Besides, as nice as Constable Patchett was, she and the squad had plenty of cases to solve, considering the spike in home burglaries over the summer. This had moved Mrs. Tomblin's case higher up the pile, but the pile was a pile, all the same.

chapter nineteen

At breakfast Matt declared today "Good Deeds Day."
"You see, kiddo," he said, as he passed me the milk to pour
on my granola (not that it was exactly a pass, more of a shuffle
– Matt's kitchen was so small that the two-seater kitchenette
table took up half the space), "Mrs. Tomblin gets to meet and
lunch with her favorite mystery writer, Paul Norman. Why all
these readers adore Norman's mysteries is—"

"A mystery," I said. That was always my line.

"But they do," he said, rolling his eyes. "And they will adore
him once again – thanks to yours truly. I came up with so many
new plot twists that I practically co-authored his new bomb
– excuse me – bomb*shell* thriller, *Secrets of Deception*. And that
hot-air title! Isn't keeping secrets one of the givens of deception?
Whatever. The marketing department likes the title. So maybe
it's not that wretched after all. Where was I going with all this?
Remind me, kiddo."

Matt swigged down his orange juice, and dug into his cereal. "Good Deeds Day!"

"Right, right. Mrs. Tomblin comes to the office with me today. I show her around, we meet Paul Norman for lunch…at a restaurant. No brown lunch bag with snakes popping out! He gets to meet a fan. Writers love to meet fans. Fans love to meet writers. Editors love to eat expense account lunches at overpriced restaurants. See, how many good deeds are done there? And there's even one for the good deed doer!"

I nodded. As we ate, Mrs. Tomblin was getting showered and dressed. These last two days she'd been happier than I'd ever seen her. To tell the truth, I had never seen her happier for longer than the time it took to relate some story about the past.

Probably a lot of things here were making her happy.

It made her happy to have someone new be fascinated by her stories.

It made her happy not to be alone for most of the day.

It made her happy to be the center of attention and to be with people who liked her.

During the day while Matt was at work, Mrs. Tomblin and I had visited the museum, lunched with Colin, and then had gone to a movie. This was turning out to be a vacation for her.

After this break at Matt's, maybe the retirement home wouldn't seem so terrible to her, after all. She was losing her house, no easy thing to lose. But at least she wouldn't be alone anymore. Hopefully she would make friends and the staff would take decent care of her.

She wasn't the only one who was happier. I was too. I didn't realize just how stressed I'd been lately with my mother and

Greg. I got out of my chair and hugged Matt clumsily. "I'm going to miss you," I said, then immediately felt like a sappy idiot.

"I'm not going anywhere, kiddo," he joked, returning the hug. "You're welcome here anytime, you know that. I always wanted a sister just like you. Can I exchange you permanently for Jonathan?"

Mrs. Tomblin came into the kitchen. She looked terrific in her floral shirtdress, pearl necklace and earrings, and beige pumps. Matt gave her a wolf whistle, then rose. "Here, you take my chair. Well, there is no other chair for you take, but we'll ignore that. Your breakfast is coming right up."

"Thank you," she said, smiling as she sat down. "You've both been so kind."

"No thanks necessary. I have the pleasure of your company and your wonderful stories. So eat up, Madam," Matt said. "A famous author awaits his biggest fan."

I started washing the dishes, while Matt went to get ready for work. The phone rang, and I heard Matt answer it. His groan told Mrs. Tomblin and me who was calling again. Richard.

"Yes, yes, I'll get your mother for you," Matt said, holding the receiver an arm's length away from his ear. I guess Richard thought that his mother had moved in with old friends who needed to be spoken to as though they were deaf and senile.

Mrs. Tomblin stood and went over to take the phone. "Yes, Richard. Yes, Richard, I know Richard. Yes, Richard, I know," she said politely.

If I had been in her place, I would have slammed down the receiver, and told Richard where to go…and it wasn't back to the beaches of Capri.

All Mrs. Tomblin had told Matt and me about these conversations was that Richard was urging her to sign off on the insurance claims. She never complained about him at all

"Yes, Richard. I know, Richard," Mrs. Tomblin said, her voice getting fainter. "Only five vintage photographs were stolen. Yes, I can still count. It was five, not all ten."

I pumped my fist in support. Mild sarcasm was as defiant as Mrs. Tomblin ever got. And only in the mornings. And only when she felt brave enough. Having Matt or me nearby for support obviously had bucked her up.

"I'm optimistic the stolen photographs will be recovered, and so I'll hold off signing the claims for the time being," Mrs. Tomblin said.

Matt, standing beside her, tapped Mrs. Tomblin's arm and signalled that she should hand him the receiver.

"Cool it, for heaven's sake! Your mother knows what she's doing and what she wants. Don't tell me it's none of my business. It's not your money yet!" Matt slammed down the receiver. "Sorry. Lost my temper there with your…son," he said apologetically.

She nodded wearily. She'd been great on the phone with him, but she didn't look too great now. Matt put his arm around her. "Go finish your breakfast and we'll leave for my office. Your favorite author awaits."

Her hands were trembling so badly that she could barely bring the spoon to her mouth. Seeing her like this made me furious, yet again, with Richard. What a pig! This was one time I wanted Mrs. Tomblin to forget, so I launched into how exciting it was going to be to spend the day with Paul Norman, having lunch, going with him and Matt to the printer to get a copy of his new book right off the press and having him autograph it for her.

After they left, I cleaned up and was getting ready for my bike tour when the phone rang again. It was that pig Richard again I assumed, snatching up the phone so fast that I didn't even check the call display. I was about to hang up when I heard, "Phoebe, it's Aunt Debbie. I called you and your mother said you had gone to stay with Matt for a few days," she said, making it sound like a question. She gave me this number."

Aunt Debbie knew my mother, boy did she. The second she'd learned I was at Matt's, she'd likely figured out what was going on. "We haven't been getting along since you guys left. I needed a break," I said bluntly.

Aunt Debbie breathed into the receiver, not needing any more explanation. She'd seen how upset I'd been by Grandy's weeping at dinner.

"Mrs. Tomblin is here too," I said, and gave her an update on the situation.

"Poor woman!" Aunt Debbie said. "Not fair at all. That son…. All I can say is what goes around comes around. He'll get his one day."

"Can it be tomorrow?" I said bitterly.

"If I had any say in the ways of the universe, you bet," Aunt Debbie said.

"How's Grandy?" I asked. I hadn't spoken to her in a few days.

"That's why I'm calling," Aunt Debbie said after a pause. "I'm concerned about her. I can't tell you how glad I am that you will be staying with her for two weeks. Keeping her company."

Whenever I asked Grandy if she was all right living alone she had repeatedly said that she had no time to be lonely. It seemed from the outside that she didn't mind. She worked part-time five days a week; and when she wasn't working she was gardening, fishing, hiking, bowling, delivering meals to house-bound seniors. At night she met up with her friends to play canasta, bridge, and poker.

But I knew she was lonely. We all knew it.

"Only a few more days and I'll be there," I said.

"Four more days," Aunt Debbie said, with a sad sort of laugh. "Grandy's counting the minutes. Your room has been prepped for weeks. And she's got enough plans to keep you both busy until next summer."

"I can't wait," I said.

I hung up and gave Grandy a call on her cell. She was at work, but so thrilled to hear from me that she didn't care, and I heard her telling her coworkers that her granddaughter was calling, and them telling her to go ahead and take her break now instead of later.

As I filled her in on what was up with Mrs. Tomblin, I could hear announcements in the background about what was on sale. "Anything you want me to get you?" Grandy asked.

I didn't need anything. I had more than I needed, thanks to Greg and Mom. It was easier for Greg to be generous with things. At first I had thought he was doing it because it was his way of showing how he felt about me, a show of affection. Well, it was, but it was also aimed at showing my mom how much he loved her by buying things for me. And sometimes it seemed as though he was buying me off, so I wouldn't make a fuss about all the attention he lavished on my mom and Elspeth.

Grandy, though, wanted to get me something to show me how much she loved and missed me and was thinking of me. So I thought hard about what I should ask for. "I need a windbreaker. I ripped mine, and you know those jeans you got me last year? They're getting too small. Are they still available? Can you get me a bigger size?"

"Is that all?" Grandy asked. "You haven't forgotten I have an employee discount."

"No way. And boy, are you're going to need it when I start shopping."

"That's a deal," Grandy said, with her familiar rumbling laugh. "Love you. See you soon."

"Love you back. Be there soon."

Two minutes later there was a ping on my BlackBerry. It was a message from Yuri.

Dear Miss Hecht, the Toronto Miss Marple,
Does the Tokyo Miss Marple have to file a missing person report on the Toronto Miss Marple? Text me ASAP or I will... to the attention of Constable Murdoch! How would you like to have him on your case? Haven't heard from you in days. I can't figure out if it's because you're too busy to fill in your Tokyo alter ego, or if it's that nada, zip, zero is the name of the crime game...Still, I am breathlessly anticipating the next chapters about the mystery of the missing photographs and the teen romance between you and Colin. ASAP, or else...you will be communicating with Constable Murdoch. And I mean chapters!!!! Details, girl!!!

Dear Miss Kimura, the Tokyo Miss Marple, Chapters? It's more like a novel! But I only have time now to give a cheat-sheet summary. Boy, could I have used your expertise at the garage sale. First, everyone looked like a possible suspect, and then nobody did. So maybe I saw him/them, who knows? I sure don't. Never thought I'd be on the lookout for criminal suspects...not like you, you mystery reader, you crime show fanatic, you devoted fan of *America's Most Wanted*.

I paused. That wasn't entirely true. After Grandy and Mom had told me about my paternal line-up and their criminal tendencies, I used to read the crime stories in the local news section on the sly and stare at pictures of any perps in the age range of my "father" to see if I resembled one of them.

As I was about to finish my text, I heard a ping. Another message from Yuri.

Hey! You still there?

I zoned out. Sorry.

You weren't zoning out, you were just building suspense in your breathless reader. How did Constable Murdoch react when you gave him the photos? He'd better have taken them as evidence. Doesn't he know Miss Marple relies on the spying eyes, overhearing ears, and gossiping tongues of the residents of St. Mary Mead to lead her to the perps?

I didn't give them to him, but to his partner. She's nicer than he is.

She! Your own Miss Marple in a police uniform!

Maybe, maybe, we'll see. Got to go!

Not for so long next time. Promise!

Promise!

Two minutes after I had finished texting, my mom called. I couldn't think what to say to her after asking how she, Elspeth and Greg were doing. My mom gave me a detailed rundown, how uncomfortable she was obvious by how she was rambling on, which was not her style at all. I didn't know how to put her at ease, or even if I wanted to.

"What have you been up to?" she asked.

"I went to a museum and a movie with Mrs. Tomblin."

"Any news about the robbery?" she asked.

"Not yet."

After a long silence, my mom said, "I forgot to tell you. I went into a toy store yesterday with Elspeth. She spotted a doll and wouldn't stop pointing and chattering until I took it off the shelf. She clutched it to herself and wouldn't let go. I had no choice but to buy it. Not just because she wanted it, since it looked like you, but she'd yanked out a handful of hair from the doll's head, so the decision was made for me."

I laughed, and Mom joined in.

"Be home soon?" she asked in a soft, hesitant voice.

"Yeah, soon," I said, my reply loaded with all the mixed emotions I was feeling about returning.

chapter twenty

A five-minute walk separated Colin's home from the Creighton manse. I'd asked Colin to come over to sort through the stash of negatives, contact sheets, and photos I'd been given by Mrs. Tomblin. On the walk from his basement apartment where I'd met up with him, I was pretty quiet, considering what a motor-mouth I was most of the time.

I was edgy about seeing my mother, especially with Colin there as witness, and about how she would respond to him. Grandy teased Mom that she was as overprotective as the most old-fashioned of grandmothers, which of course, Grandy most definitely was not. The few boys I dated back in Barrie had been cross-examined by my mother with the zeal of one of those prosecution lawyers you see in crime shows. Colin had nothing to hide, and from watching him debate, I knew he would be able to hold his own. Yet I grew more stressed by the second, as we went up the walkway toward the house.

Colin was excited about seeing Rachel Malick's contact sheets. So excited, fortunately for me, he was doing most of the talking, with me tossing in the occasional question.

After Colin's crash course in photography and some web sleuthing on the subject, I'd been able to start the sorting process. Even I had been able to figure out that the professional contact sheets containing rows and rows of mini prints had been made by Rachel Malick.

Sorting out the negatives was a whole other matter. Colin said that he would be able to recognize, by the size and type of negative, which belonged to Mrs. Tomblin's photos and which to Rachel Malick's, so we could hand over Malick's to the curator at the art gallery. As Colin sorted through the negatives, I was going to continue with some sorting of my own. I was going through Mrs. Tomblin's albums to make (as best as I could) one highlight album for her to take with her to Meadowrest. As I had promised, I would hold on to the others for her.

It was turning out to be harder than I had assumed. And not merely for the obvious reason that I wasn't Mrs. Tomblin. Aside from the standard ones like wedding and honeymoon pictures, pictures of Richard as a baby and toddler (not as an adult!) and those of family celebrations, only she would know which were the highlights. A "looks-like-nothing-out-of-the-ordinary-moment" could be a highlight as much as a wedding photo. There was a photo of Grandy and me, for instance, that I absolutely loved, taken by Aunt Debbie.

Wearing dopey-looking sun hats, we were on our knees, side by side, replanting Grandy's front flower bed. She was holding tulip bulbs in one hand, a spade in other, her elbows and hands covered with dirt. I had turned my head to look at her, while taking a break from digging. It seemed like just another ordinary moment, but it wasn't. Not for me. Grandy made everything a fun team sport. Since it was "our garden" I could plant what I wanted where I wanted. So I had. Sometimes with good results. Sometimes not.

But she let me learn how to figure stuff out myself. So that "ordinary" picture of Grandy and me, spades in hands, straw hats on head, was a highlight. A major favorite.

As I'd leafed through Mrs. Tomblin's albums, I'd tried my best to choose ones that would make her happy to remember. I'd gotten depressed doing it. Many of the people she had known and loved were dead or seemed to have drifted out of her life. Having Alzheimer's, eventually Mrs. Tomblin might not be able even to recognize any of those people who had meant so much to her.

Before I knew it, we were at my house. "Here we are," I said, probably sounding as though I had arrived at the dentist to have a root canal or something equally painful. Colin gave me a look, but didn't say anything. Then. Or a minute later, when instead of opening the door with my key, I knocked as a stranger would have.

Mom answered the door with a sleeping Elspeth in her arms.

"Hi Mom," I said, my voice a bit jittery.

"Phoebe," she said sounding equally strained. She stepped closer and leaned over Elspeth to kiss me.

"Mom, this is my friend Colin Flanagan. Colin, this is my mother and this is my adorable half-sister Elspeth," I said.

"Sister," my mother corrected.

Touched, I kissed her on the cheek and Elspeth on the head. Mom stroked Elspeth's hair. "What a sleeper she is. Not like Phoebe. Two hours max and Phoebe was awake and raring to go. She'd grab hold of the crib bars and rattle them, telling me she wanted to be picked up to go some place new. Immediately. If I didn't rush over, she then told me at the top of her lungs I needed to pick up my speed. And once she could walk, that crib became a mini-gym, with Phoebe practicing jumps and stretches on the mattress and bars." She paused, her voice suddenly petering out, and glanced apprehensively at me, as if she might have embarrassed me. But I'd been begging her for months to do what she had just done – acknowledge the good parts of our past.

"I'm still like that, huh?" I smiled, trying to support her, to show how grateful I was. And I was, but I remained jumpy too, as we all seemed to be, standing there, darting gazes and smiling nervously at each other.

Then Elspeth woke up and seeing me, made noises that sounded like "Febe" and stretched her hands toward my hair. "I guess she wants the real thing," my mom said, smiling, though still a bit apprehensively.

Before Elspeth could yank out a handful of the real thing, I tickled her hand, making her let go. "How's my little sis?" I asked, and took Elspeth from my mother's arms. "Miss me? I missed you!" I said, carefully raising her up and down, which she always enjoyed.

"Febe!" She giggled, placing her hands on my face.

Jiggling Elspeth, I said, "Mom, Colin's here to help me sort through Mrs. Tomblin's photos."

Suddenly Elspeth was squirming so much I could barely hold onto her. I patted her bottom and figured out why. "Want me to change her?" I asked.

"No, no, you just got home," Mom said. "I can do it."

"I don't mind, really," I said. "You probably need a break from diaper duty. What is that Grandy always says about babies? Spittle, drool, vomit, and you know the rest. More comes out of a baby than goes in."

Mom laughed along with Colin.

Grandy, Aunt Debbie, and my mom had supported each other like a tag team raising Adam, Chris, and me, pitching in when one of them had to go to work or needed a break. Now I belonged to that tag team, I realized. "Be back in a few minutes," I said.

As I was cleaning and diapering Elspeth, I heard Mom ask Colin where he went to school. When he answered Lytton Academy, she said, "Outstanding school, isn't it?" By now she was familiar with all the top schools in Toronto, as she was about a whole slew of other "tops" – thanks to Greg's relentless input.

Back in Barrie, she'd read *Vogue* and *InStyle*, so she was already up on the top designers and the season's hottest fashion items. After Greg's lecture series, she also knew which were the best wines, food shops, appliances, restaurants, electronics, and vacation spots.

As I came back into the living room rocking a contented, sleepy Elspeth, my mother was questioning Colin about his parents and what they did.

"My da, he's the superintendent at the Excelsior apartment

on Avenue Road. My ma helps him out, and then there's my three younger brothers to take care of. My two older sisters chip in too," he said.

"That's nice," my mom said shyly. "My sister and mother helped me with Phoebe when she was growing up. I worked, and I really appreciated the extra hands, as I am sure your parents do."

"What work did you do?" Colin asked.

If a heart could sink to knee level, that was where mine was heading. I hoped that question didn't make my mother slam and dead bolt the door to her past, which she had been slowly creaking open.

"Every job you can do in a restaurant except cook," she said after a long pause. "Fruit, vegetable, dish, and pot washer, table setter, waitress, hostess, and restaurant manager."

Colin nodded as she spoke. "My da says you need to know how to do a bit of everything to be a good super. I bet all that helped you be a good manager," he said.

"It did," my mom said softly.

As Colin continued to ask interested questions about her work, I could see her battling to keep that door to the past open. I wanted to go over and hug her because I knew how hard it was for her, even with Colin, whose background was similar to ours.

Though there were some doors to the past that were locked for good reason and could stay that way for all I cared, there were many that led to happy memories that I hoped my mom would eventually be able to share. Talking with Colin was a great first step.

"Elspeth's falling asleep again," I said as I handed her over to Mom. "Maybe you should put her in her crib."

She nodded. "After I put her to bed, I'll join you in your room. I fixed up a few things for you."

Startled was hardly the word to describe my reaction. What was there to fix up in my room? Mom went into Elspeth's nursery and Colin and I headed for my room.

In one of the rare moments in my life, I was truly speechless when I entered my room and saw what my mother had done. She'd framed the family photos I'd printed out in antique-style gold leaf frames, remembering how much I liked Grandy's ornate frames, and she'd put the photos of Mrs. Tomblin that I'd tucked under the border of my dresser mirror into standing acrylic frames.

"Do you like it?" my mom asked, looking anxiously at me as she entered. "I chose antique frames because I know you don't like those metallic modern ones, and I put Mrs. Tomblin's in those acrylic frames because the corners were curling and I thought it would straighten them up. You like it, I hope."

I started to cry and stood there heaving to control myself. My mom hurried over me and held me close. "Thanks. It's wonderful. The frames are beautiful. And those acrylic frames are a great idea for Mrs. Tomblin's pictures. My room looks like an art gallery."

I could see that she was pleased and as she turned to leave, I tapped her on the arm and asked, "Do you want to stay and help us go through all this stuff?"

She blushed, not as one of her too-frequent displays of embarrassment, but with joy. "I'd be glad to. I don't know much though; you'll have to show me what to do."

"Colin will give you a quick crash course, like he did me," I said. "You'll pick it up faster than I did. You're a brilliant student. I should be so brilliant."

"You will be," she said.

I went over to the closet and took out the box. We sat down on the carpet and chatted as we sorted. This was one of those looks-like-nothing-special moments to anyone else, but it was a highlight – a huge one.

chapter twenty-one

I was out in the garage shed behind Mrs. Tomblin's house. Camping outdoors, even with mosquitoes, black flies, bees and creepy crawlies, sure beat sitting on a borrowed kitchen chair by a dirt-encrusted window in a dark, damp garage shed, surrounded by stinking bags of mulch and fertilizer.

I wondered if Miss Marple had done anything like this. If she had, it would have cured her of her interest in solving mysteries. It was curing mine.

Two hours into the stakeout, and I was getting as buggy as the bugs I was swatting and slapping off. Without them, though, and the regular pinging of my BlackBerry with messages from Yuri (who was camped out in front of her laptop), I probably would have fallen asleep long ago. It was that boring watching the back of the house with a pair of Colin's binoculars through the few clear streaks of the dirty window. Good thing it was dirty, though. I didn't want to be waving the binoculars in greeting to the burglars, should they ever turn up.

Another good thing about being so bored was I was too bored to even be scared a little. I had seen how badly they'd beaten up Mrs. Tomblin. Even though I'm athletic and stronger than she was, still I'd bet two bags of mulch and raise you a bag of fertilizer that the burglars could floor me too.

I did have a weapon of a sort to defend myself with – a can of extra-hold hairspray. I'd bought the same brand Grandy used. It wasn't as eye-burning as pepper spray, but pretty close, in my opinion. Every time Grandy sprayed her hair, I had to open the window before I could use the bathroom.

Where *were* those burglars? Didn't they know that this was their last chance? And our last chance to catch them in the act?

They should know. Since Mrs. Tomblin, Colin, and I had been blabbing away to everyone at the garage sale, there couldn't be anyone in the neighborhood who didn't know that there were still Malick photographs in the house, and that movers were coming to take Mrs. Tomblin's things to storage tomorrow morning.

So come and get it, burglars! They would "get" their pictures taken! I had Colin's camera, along with the binoculars. Colin was joining me after his shift, and if we didn't catch them in action, there was the security camera he had installed in the living room yesterday. His boss had let Colin borrow one from the store. Mrs. Tomblin had been a regular customer for years, and he wanted "those sons of guns" who'd beaten her up arrested.

Me too. Especially after that terrible scene last night.

Yesterday Richard had not stopped calling. Mrs. Tomblin

had spoken to him twice, repeatedly insisting she wouldn't sign the insurance claim forms. He hadn't given up though, and kept on calling. Matt had finally disconnected the phone and we'd taken Mrs. Tomblin to dinner to distract her.

It had almost worked. When we got back to Matt's, she had seemingly forgotten all about Richard's harassing phone calls and name-calling. Then he'd shown up mid-evening at Matt's door, flowers in one hand and candies in the other, on a charm offensive obviously.

Matt and I both found his "charm" offensive and as fake as a forgery. While I stood guard, Matt went to tell Mrs. Tomblin that her son was here and ask if she wanted to see him. She was already in bed and said that she was too exhausted now – perhaps tomorrow.

When Matt relayed that to Richard, he looked ready to smash the box of candies in Matt's face. Matt whispered that I should go into the bedroom, close the door, and turn on the radio. I did, blasting Bach and Mozart, hoping that that was all Mrs. Tomblin could hear and not the quarrelling going on between Matt and Richard.

Even a booming Beethoven symphony couldn't drown out their rising voices. I opened the door and peeked out to see Richard waving his arms and shouting. He looked hyped-up enough to attempt a home invasion.

"It's time for you to leave," Matt said. "In fact, your departure is long overdue!"

"Don't you dare tell me what to do!"

Why didn't Matt just slam the door in his face? I would have. But Richard was standing right in the doorframe and knowing him, he'd sue Matt for causing bodily harm if Matt tried to slam the door. Surprisingly, Richard didn't say he was going to call the police if Matt laid a finger on him.

I heard a door open and the voice of Mrs. Witherspoon, the hall monitor, as Matt called her. He swore that Mrs. Witherspoon sat on a chair by her door on the lookout for residents who didn't push their garbage completely down the chute, or who didn't carry their pets out of the building – no dog or cat feet were allowed on the carpeting. She kept an eye on (more like spied on) who was coming and going, and who was visiting whom.

"Gentlemen," Mrs. Witherspoon called out. "You have disturbed the peace sufficiently this evening. One more word of argument from either of you and I am telephoning the police."

"Please do me a favor and make that call pronto," Matt sang out. "And please ask for Constable Murdoch! He's on the case already."

The mention of Constable Murdoch's name instantly quieted Richard. Did he have a police phobia or something? I was tempted to dash over and hiss "Constable Murdoch" to see how far and how fast he'd run.

"You'll be hearing from my lawyers!" Richard sputtered and hustled off.

Matt apologized to Mrs. Witherspoon, explaining the circumstances. Besides being on garbage and pet patrol, there was nothing Mrs. Witherspoon loved more than the inside scoop. Matt calmed her down by giving her some, and building her sympathy for Mrs. Tomblin.

He came in, shut the door, and leaned against it, breathing hard. "'How sharper than a serpent's tooth it is, to have a thankless child!' Shakespeare knew what he was talking about, didn't he? A python has nothing on that poor excuse for a man!"

The whole scene had made a wreck of Mrs. Tomblin, reviving all her guilty feelings. She came into the living room and went on and on about the photos and her promise to her aunt and how she'd broken it by being selfish and possessive about the photographs. It was just that they brought back so many happy memories, she said, feeling she had to explain again why she had held onto them. Nothing Matt or I could say or do could stop her from repeating all that over and over until she'd worn herself out. I sat beside her bed holding her hand until she finally fell asleep.

Matt and I hadn't been able to get to sleep, though. We were too restless. We watched a TV talk show and then this comic western called *Cat Ballou*. Eventually we both nodded off on the couch where we were woken up in the morning by Mrs. Tomblin. She seemed to have forgotten most of last evening, which was good in a horrible way, but we hadn't.

I wanted to try to get those photos back so Mrs. Tomblin could stop feeling so terrible about breaking her promise to her aunt. In between swatting off bugs and peeking out the window, I was texting Yuri, hoping all this activity would keep me awake.

Another BlackBerry ping.

> Another wake-up call from your human alarm clock. You *are* awake?

How could I not be with all this texting! When my fingers aren't flipping off bugs, they're texting you...you human pest, you...not that I'm not grateful for pests, insect and human. How do cops and security guards stand it...all the watching and waiting. They must almost want some crime to go down, just so they can feel that they are doing their job, and not wasting their time. I can't decide what I am more afraid of – the burglars showing up or nothing happening. Let me tell you, sitting still is hard work.

Especially for girl athletes!

Like you are so good at sitting still. Remember, I sat next to you in lectures and class. When you weren't straightening your skirt, you were flicking lint off your sweater, and picking at your nail polish.

Ha! Ha! I was just doing you a favor…acting out your excess nervous energy. Okay, probably that explanation doesn't work for you. How about when I was transmitting my energy to you to keep you from going into a coma during the lectures. How about a bit of both?

Some creepy-crawly crawled onto my BlackBerry, and while swatting the bug off, I dropped it. When I picked it up, there was another message.

> See something?

> Just more insect vermin, no human ones yet.

> Your human criminal vermin are on the way, Madame Yuri sees it in the stars.

> I hear a noise, get back to you later, Madame Yuri.

I listened intently as I peeked through the streaky window. The noise was only the neighbor's backyard water sprinkler hitting the metal side of the garage shed.

Another half hour passed and my only in-person company continued to be the flies, mosquitoes, and ants that wanted me out of their space. The insect repellent I'd put on earlier was no longer working. I must have sweated it off, and I swear I needed as many blades as a windmill to swat off my buggy companions.

I heard footsteps and my heart started to thump in rhythm with the steps. I quickly put the binoculars on the chair beside me and grabbed the camera and the can of hairspray. With one hand I aimed the camera through one of the clear streaks, and with the other, I aimed the hairspray nozzle in the direction of the door.

"Hey, don't spray me! I'm innocent, I swear!" It was Colin. I didn't realize how scared I'd been until I slumped with relief at seeing him.

"That's quite the weapon," he kidded, tapping the can. "Are you going to spray them into place until the police come to arrest them?"

"Very funny! I was going to use it like pepper spray. Blind them so I could make a quick escape. Your hair could use a little spray," I teased, aiming the can at his head. His thick black hair was all over the place, as usual. "I'll be kind this time; I'll just smooth it down with my hand."

And that's what I did. He looked at me, and I looked back at him. I wasn't thinking about burglars. Neither was he from the way he was looking at me. We'd never catch the burglars staring at each other. He knew that too.

"You want me to handle the binoculars or the camera?" he asked.

"Camera," I said. "You're the expert." I handed it over to him.

All I continued to see through the binoculars were the streaks of dirt on the window, magnified. Every five minutes I'd put them down and give my eyes a rest…by gazing at Colin who was staring out the window as if he sensed the burglars were going to show their sorry selves very soon.

Despite all my fantasies about Colin as I mooned over him at school and stalked him by bike, I'd never really believed that any of them would come true. What had come true was more than I would have believed. He'd become a good friend. I was as comfortable with him as I was with Yuri and my cousins. I couldn't wait to give Yuri the lowdown in person, and have her give me the lowdown on what she thought of me and Colin together.

"Hey, look who's here!" Colin said, peering through the binoculars he'd taken off my lap. He handed them back to me.

"The hosers! Why am I not surprised?"

It was the moron who'd kept winking at me and his equally moronic BFF, Gary, Mrs. Tomblin's old paperboy. Now he would know the outside of her house, and how to get in. "Those are the guys from the garage sale!" Colin whispered, snapping shots as they sauntered into the backyard carting two big, black carrying cases.

As Colin snapped away, the Winker picked the lock on the back door as quickly and efficiently as an experienced locksmith…or experienced burglar. Lock picked, they casually went inside as though they'd used a key to enter their own place. Not morons after all, I thought.

I grabbed my BlackBerry and called 911. "I just saw two guys breaking into a house. Here's the address. How do I know? I am watching them. Why I am watching them? I'll explain to the police when they arrive. Just send someone. The lady who lives here – Mrs. Tomblin – was already robbed once and beaten up."

How much more explanation did this 911 operator want? These guys would be long gone by the time I got her to send the police. At last she seemed convinced and told me a squad car would arrive shortly.

"Do you think they planned this on their own?" I whispered to Colin.

He shook his head. "Art thieves need to have an international network of contacts to get the art out of the country and to prospective buyers. I'm guessing these two would never know how much a Malick photograph was worth unless someone told them. They are working for someone."

It was a bright, sunny afternoon. How did they think they were going to carry out the photos they'd come to steal with the neighbors out and about? There had to be a third person, probably the driver of their getaway car watching nearby, ready to help if they needed it.

"There's somebody else with them, isn't there?" I asked Colin, suddenly getting panicky. "He could be anywhere. Close enough even to see us."

Colin nodded. "We should duck under the window. We've got all the proof we need."

So we ducked. We waited on the dusty floor, each minute feeling like an hour, each minute ending with the sound of one of us slapping a leg or an arm to get another bug off.

The local police division was less than five minutes away by car. Where were those cops? Maybe the 911 operator hadn't taken me seriously after all – had thought I was some crank caller.

"The cops aren't going to show up!" I muttered.

"If they don't," Colin said, "at least we have the pictures."

Those photos would just be added to Mrs. Tomblin's file in the huge pile of files on recent burglaries, I thought, becoming dejected. This was all for nothing.

I heard something. The police? Colin and I got up and peeked through the lowest streak on the window. Entering the backyard was a person I never, ever believed I would be overjoyed to see – Constable Murdoch, followed by Constable Patchett and two other constables.

They huddled together, and then Murdoch and Patchett went in the back door, and the other two constables hurried out of the backyard, probably to prevent the Winker and Gary from exiting through the front.

We heard shouting and furniture hitting the ground. I glanced at Colin, who looked as worried as I was. Those two were mean and violent and would resist arrest – maybe even with weapons. There was more yelling, banging and scuffling, and I prayed that the constables wouldn't get injured.

"Don't do anything stupid! Drop it right now!" Constable Murdoch yelled. "You're in enough trouble as it is!" There was more yelling and banging and suddenly there was quiet.

"Hands up in the air where I can see them!" Constable Patchett said loudly. "Now, place them behind your backs. Move along."

A few minutes later the other two constables exited through the back door. Murdoch and Patchett must be taking the Winker and Gary out the front. Soon afterwards, one of the constables returned and applied crime-scene tape between the railings on the first porch step.

"The forensic team is on the way," I whispered.

We heard police sirens, car tires squealing, and new voices. It was over for the Winker and Gary. Though considering what Colin had told me about art theft, the stolen photographs could be anywhere in the world. Who knew if they could be tracked down and retrieved?

"Good work, Miss Marple," Colin said, wrapping an arm around me.

"Good work, Monsieur Poirot," I replied with a sigh, hoping all this paid off with Mrs. Tomblin getting the photos back.

chapter twenty-two

"This was the key to the case," Constable Patchett said, pointing to one of the photos Colin had taken at the garage sale. She had invited Colin and me over to the station to fill us in, as much as she could, without compromising the case. She'd ordered in a gourmet pizza and soft drinks, which she and I were demolishing. Colin had cancelled, having to go to work instead, to cover for an employee who'd called in sick.

I stared at the picture. Who would have guessed – not me, not ever – that this was anything out of the ordinary. It was just a shot of a guy in his forties, smoking a cigarette, leaning against a car parked across the street from Mrs. Tomblin's. But it had cracked the case. Every photo, it seemed, had a story behind it, like a cover illustration on a Christie mystery, full of clues.

"That's Tommy Garvey," Constable Patchett said, tapping a fingernail on the photo. "He's well-known to the police. Been arrested several times, but none of the charges have stuck. Until now." She crossed her fingers.

"What's he been arrested for?"

"When I worked in Property and Evidence Management, I assisted on a case in which Tommy Garvey was suspected of arranging the theft of a museum-quality antique French clock, made of porcelain, gold, and bronze. It was worth over a hundred thousand dollars. Not the easiest thing to fence or to find a buyer for without the international contacts that Tommy Garvey has built up over the years. It was recovered after it was sold at an auction with a forged provenance – the provenance documents the history of its ownership. The buyer checked out the provenance and contacted Interpol. There were so many links in the international theft chain that the Toronto police and Interpol couldn't make the charges stick against Tommy. Not that time."

She gave the photo a final tap, like she was positively identifying a perp in a police lineup. "This picture was the game changer. When I showed it to Constable Murdoch we decided we could no longer work on the assumption that the robbery at Mrs. Tomblin's had been random. It was too much of a coincidence that Tommy Garvey was hanging around a house recently robbed of very valuable photographs."

So how did a big-time master thief and fence like Tommy Garvey hook up with hosers like the Winker and Gary the paperboy? I stared at a shot of the three of them by the car and another of the Winker and Gary standing by a display table on the driveway. What was the connection? I picked up the photos to examine them close up.

The Winker and Gary's heads were turned toward Tommy

Garvey. They had similar long faces and huge square jaws topped by already-starting-to-recede hairlines. The nearly identical square jaw clamping down on a cigarette belonged to Tommy Garvey and his hairline had receded right to the back of his head.

"These two hosers are related to Tommy Garvey, aren't they? You can see the family resemblance."

Constable Patchett nodded. "You're good at picking up clues."

"I've had plenty of practice this summer," I said, sighing.

She gave me a curious look, but didn't probe. "They are Tommy's nephews, Brian and Gary Garvey. Their rap sheets show that they usually work on their own, but I guess Tommy's regular crew was either on vacation or in jail, so they've been breaking into houses he targets. All three of them know the Tomblins. Tommy went to the same high school as Richard Tomblin."

After only a week, the police knew a great deal about the case. In the Agatha Christie mysteries I've read (five down, seventy-five to go) and the TV crime series I watched, it took Miss Marple, police detectives, and forensic experts repeated questioning to get to even the beginnings of the truth. That was always followed by tough bargaining with criminal defense lawyers to get plea agreements so that the suspects would finally tell the whole truth and nothing but the truth.

"How do you know so much already?" I blurted out. Realizing that my question might appear insulting, I quickly added, "I'm awed."

Constable Patchett smiled and shrugged. "Everything and

everybody just fell into place." Then she launched into the long-ish short version for me.

The detectives investigating the stolen clock case had discovered a direct link to Tommy Garvey and were ready to charge him. The driver of the van parked in front of Mrs. Tomblin's house was a known associate of Garvey's, and the van had been rented by Tommy.

The fact that the van was full of break-in tools and stolen property – Blu-ray players, iPhones and iPods, laptops, and net-books – had enabled the police to obtain a search warrant for Garvey's home and storage lockers. In one of the lockers, along with other stolen goods, the police had found one of the Malick photographs.

Following the arrests of the Garvey clan, the squealing and finger pointing had started immediately. A square jaw was a family trait; loyalty apparently wasn't, Constable Patchett said.

The result was that Brian and Gary were being charged with aggravated assault, a serious crime with considerable prison time attached, for their vicious beating of Mrs. Tomblin, in addition to several robbery charges.

To get Tommy talking, the detectives had threatened to charge him, not merely with theft, the criminal possession of stolen goods, and forgery, but as an accessory to the assault. To reduce the length of his prison sentence and its conditions, he'd given up Brian and Gary, admitting he'd hired his nephews to steal the photographs.

"Wow!" I sat back in the chair, feeling thrilled that Yuri, Colin and I had helped close the case. I couldn't wait to get home to call Colin and text Yuri. My fingers were going to be permanently crabbed from texting her the facts of the case, which were as detailed as the final chapter in any Agatha Christie mystery. I could wait until she got home in two days, but knowing Yuri, and appreciating all of her most excellent Miss Marple guidance and advice, I figured she deserved to be told ASAP who'd done it and why. Besides, I'd never hear the end of it, if I didn't tell all.

"Case closed, huh!"

"Not quite yet," Constable Patchett said slowly, putting down the third slice of pizza she'd been about to eat. "You've been a good friend to Mrs. Tomblin, and I'm sorry to have to tell you this last part. Tommy Garvey claims he was hired by Richard Tomblin to arrange the theft of the Malick photographs and then to fence them to several collectors in Monaco and France. Garvey was to get twenty-five percent of the profit of the sales. E-mails and text messages seem to back up his assertion. So do his phone records, which show a high volume of calls between his and Richard Tomblin's cell phones. Forensic accountants are analyzing the financial trail."

I felt sick. Sick enough to throw up. I stood up suddenly, heaving, frantically looking around for a garbage container. I saw one in the corner and made it just in time. I felt Constable Patchett's hand on my back. She handed me a napkin to wipe my mouth and helped me back to the table.

"I guess that creep couldn't stand the idea that what remained of his 'inheritance' was being donated to the art gallery. This way the money from the collectors and the insurance money would have been his, once Mrs. Tomblin died," I said bitterly. "Even before maybe, since Mrs. Tomblin has Alzheimer's – you know that."

"I do," she said quietly. "I've been in touch with her neighbors and relatives."

"Giving up Richard's involvement must be another part of Tommy's plea bargain, I suppose. Glad for that, at least," I muttered. The potential charges Richard faced included scheming to defraud, falsifying business and bank records, conspiracy, and accessory to theft. Of course, he was denying it all.

Then it struck me that Mrs. Tomblin had given (or had been badgered into giving) Richard power of attorney. "I bet he's already got his paws on his mother's money," I said angrily. "Like the money for the sale of the house. He has power of attorney; I bet he's been taking advantage of her Alzheimer's, treating her money as if it were his already."

"That is a concern," Constable Patchett said carefully. "The prosecutor assigned to the case has informed Mrs. Tomblin of Richard's potential involvement in the theft and other matters. For her legal protection, she was advised to sign documents taking away Richard's power of attorney. Mrs. Tomblin did that yesterday."

I could barely nod my head. "I'm going to see Mrs. Tomblin later this afternoon," I said. I could just imagine how terrible she must feel after being informed of Richard's involvement.

"Two of the photographs have been recovered," the constable continued. "One buyer. And then there's the one the police recovered in Garvey's storage locker. That's some good news you can tell Mrs. Tomblin. We are also reasonably confident about recovering the others. Tommy gave us the names of the buyers, and Interpol is searching for them. You did a good job, remember that! I know it doesn't seem like it. Thanks to you, Mrs. Tomblin is now going to be protected from her son. She has a second cousin that she is close to, Linda Kennison. Mrs. Kennison is coming to Toronto to be with her."

The wedding of Linda Kennison's daughter in St. Catharines was where Mrs. Tomblin was supposed to have been the weekend of the robbery.

"Mrs. Tomblin is fortunate to have you and Colin as friends," Constable Patchett continued. "Without that picture Colin took, we wouldn't have gotten wind of Tommy Garvey's involvement. And without your 911 call, we wouldn't have caught them in the act. You're fortunate too. You and Colin could have been hurt. So..." she bent her head close to mine and whispered, "For your own safety, please leave the detecting to the police next time."

I nodded wearily.

"Give my best regards to Mrs. Tomblin. And I'll say it one more time. You did a good job!"

I shrugged. I knew Colin and I done a good thing, but I didn't feel good. I felt sick. I felt like crying and yelling at the same time, and I knew Colin would be just as upset, once I filled him in. I shook the constable's hand and got up to leave.

Mrs. Tomblin would be getting back the photographs to give to the gallery – all of them, hopefully. But she had lost faith that she had the kind of son she wanted. I didn't think even the recovery of her beloved photographs could make up for that.

chapter twenty-three

I had assumed that the solving of the crime was a happy occasion, not as happy an occasion as a wedding at the end of a romantic movie, but close.

It wasn't like that in real life. It wasn't even like that in many mysteries either, according to Yuri's latest text message.

Often the criminal was someone everybody knew. That was easy to believe in the Agatha Christie mysteries, since Miss Marple lived in the tiny village of St. Mary Mead where everybody knew everybody. The murderer, thief, swindler, or kidnapper was usually someone Miss Marple knew well or resembled somebody she knew well, and that resemblance led her straight to the perp.

That meant you could be living right next to someone you thought you knew, but really didn't. Someone you might have thought was a trustworthy person, but wasn't. Even if you didn't think someone was trustworthy, you still didn't think he or she was as awful as he or she proved to be.

That was often the case in big cities too, where you'd see a news report about a hit-and-run driver described by his shocked neighbors as a devoted family man, after he'd zoomed off, leaving some poor pedestrian unconscious and bleeding on the street. As Constable Patchett had told me, in many cases, people learned things about friends they knew and family they loved that were painful to face. It was a good thing that a mystery was solved and the criminal went to prison. Yet, a good thing wasn't always a happy thing.

Those thoughts kept replaying in my head as I biked over to see Mrs. Tomblin at the retirement home. I was dreading it. I really cared for her and I was hoping that the photo album I was bringing and the acrylic framed pictures from my mom would cheer her up. My backpack was as heavy as a suitcase, bulging with a box of chocolate truffles, a pack of assorted teas, a tin of triple chocolate chip cookies and a bottle of honey.

Still, how could any of those things make up for what she had learned about her son? The weight of my backpack was slowing me down. The dread was too. Constable Patchett told me that when Mrs. Tomblin had been informed about Richard's possible involvement, all she'd said was, "I know, I know."

What did she mean by "I know, I know?"

She knew Richard well enough not to call him when she was in the hospital, beaten up by the creeps he'd hired to steal her photographs. She knew he wouldn't come back from his vacation to help her. She knew him well enough not to give in when Richard had been relentlessly hounding her to sign the insurance claims. Whatever he'd said, she wouldn't sign her name to a claim that wasn't truthful.

Put all that together and whether you were Mrs. Tomblin, Constable Patchett, Colin, or me, it wasn't a shocking revelation that Richard was behind the robbery. The clues had all been there. The "coincidence" of his being on vacation at the time of the robbery – couldn't get a better alibi than that, he supposed (wrongly, as it turned out for the big creep). His odd jumpiness at the mention of the police. The highballed insured value of the contents of the house. His insistence that his mother sign the claims so it would seem that he had no ties to the case and the insurance money.

I locked my bike up at a stand a block from the retirement home and headed over. From the outside when I reached it, the Meadowrest looked like an okay place. Built of yellow brick, it appeared no different than the other older, low-rise apartments on the block. Inside was another matter. First thing that hit me was the smell – a combination of the damp, musty odor that you smelled in old motels and the stinging smell of various cleaning products.

Wheelchairs and walkers were lined up against the back wall of the lobby. Lobby didn't seem to be the right word, since what it resembled was a waiting area in a hospital. It had the same uncomfortable metal chairs and tables with piles of newspapers and magazines. There was a glassed-in station near the elevators and I went there first to get directions to Mrs. Tomblin's suite.

"She's certainly getting a lot of visitors," the receptionist said.

That was encouraging to hear.

"Everyone gets a lot of visitors at the beginning," the receptionist went on. What she was really saying was that once the person settled in, hardly anyone came to visit anymore. I promised myself to keep visiting Mrs. Tomblin regularly. Colin and Matt would too, for sure, and I hoped Linda Kennison and Mrs. Tomblin's neighbors would as well.

As I went up two flights of stairs, I wondered what shape Mrs. Tomblin would be in today. Her memory had been pretty bad when I'd spoken to her on the phone last night. She asked me how Matt was, and I told her. Two questions later, she asked me again how Matt was, and I repeated my answer. Then she kept dropping the phone receiver, going off to search for her reading glasses, which she couldn't find. As I waited on the line, I heard the sound of drawers opening and closing and her talking to herself. Suddenly I remembered that she kept a spare pair of glasses in her purse. When she came back to the phone, all upset about not finding them, I reminded her about the spares. I thought that would put her at ease, but it didn't. She was obsessed with finding the other pair, and she hung up to continue looking for them. I tried calling back, but the line was busy. She must have put the receiver down incorrectly.

At Matt's, you would hardly have known she was in the early stages of Alzheimer's. Having us around seemed to calm and reassure her. It was nice to see how contented she'd been to have company to eat with, watch television with, talk to.

Perhaps having company here would be calming and reassuring once she started to feel at home. The floor she was living on was for residents mostly able to take care of themselves. The suites on it were small apartments. The top three floors, however, had rooms like those in a hospital ward for the residents unable to care for themselves.

Standing in the hallway next to Mrs. Tomblin's room was a caregiver in a blue uniform talking to a tall, middle-aged woman with short, streaked blond hair. Her voice was familiar. It was Linda Kennison. She'd called a few times while Mrs. Tomblin was staying at Matt's.

"Mrs. Kennison," I called out. She turned to look at me. Her face was familiar too. She was in a number of the photos I'd included in the album for Mrs. Tomblin.

"Phoebe!" she said, smiling at me. "We meet at last."

I stood back, waiting for her to finish talking with the caregiver, and then I went over.

"Thank you for everything you've done for Leah," she said, her voice breaking. "God only knows what could have happened."

"But it didn't," I said, not wanting to think about it.

She nodded. "I blame myself. I got so wrapped up in the arrangements and planning of my daughter's wedding. I used to come weekly to Toronto to be with her. She was close to my mother, who was her cousin. They grew up together. However, I haven't visited her the last two months. If I had been around…"

Her feeling guilty was a good sign that she genuinely cared for Mrs. Tomblin, and that Mrs. Tomblin could rely on her. "How is she today?" I asked. "Did she say anything about Richard?"

Mrs. Tomblin never talked much about unhappy personal things with me. She seemed to be a private person and proud, too. Maybe with Mrs. Kennison she would be able to share her feelings about Richard being the one behind all this. That could help her get past it. Though it was difficult to imagine getting past what Richard had done. I kept thinking about Mrs. Tomblin repeating, "I know, I know." Did that "knowing" make it any easier to take all this in?

Mrs. Kennison shook her head. "Leah won't talk about him. I gave it a try, but she keeps changing the subject. Better that way, likely. What is there to say about Richard anyway? He's unspeakable."

I had a few choice things to say about Richard. Actually, I had a lot of choice things to say about what a lowlife he was. If ears could burn, his would have burnt to a crisp and flaked off by now.

"Your friend Colin is with Leah," Mrs. Kennison said. "One of the social workers told us that making the suite homey will make her adjustment smoother. When I left, he was hanging up pictures. I'm going out to buy a few things Leah needs. Glad to meet you, Phoebe, and thank you again for all you have done for Leah." She shook my hand and left.

I paused outside Mrs. Tomblin's room, still slightly dreading seeing her. "No, a bit higher and to the right," Mrs. Tomblin said. "Yes, yes, there!"

Colin was on a stepladder hanging up a small reprint of one of Malick's photographs. The wall behind the couch was like a mini-exhibit of her work. How had Colin been able to do that? Mrs. Tomblin was sitting in a wing chair, her feet up, and she looked…if not as happy as she'd been at Matt's, nearer to that than what I'd been fearing.

"Phoebe, look what Colin's doing for me! He's such a nice boy."

Colin glanced at me and smiled. I felt like running over and hugging him. Later I'd do that. Later. "He *is* a nice boy!" I teased, and Colin flushed.

"You're wondering about all the additional reprints, Miss Marple," he said. "One of the photography curators made them for Mrs. Tomblin in appreciation for her donation. The gallery is organizing a traveling exhibition and using the reprints to plan out how the photographs are to be displayed."

I went over to Mrs. Tomblin and rested my left hand on her shoulder. "I have chocolates and cookies for you to eat while you instruct your personal curator where to hang the photos." She smiled at me as I gave her what I'd brought in my backpack. She examined everything with delight.

The suite wasn't bad at all. Not like her house, but not bad. There was a bedroom off to the side, a galley kitchen, and the small living and dining room area we were in now.

I handed her the photo album and the standing frames. "I made this for you. It's an album of the top hits of the photos you gave me for safekeeping. And my mom, she got these frames for your pictures."

"Thank you, and please give my thanks to your mother. It was very kind of her," she said softly, placing the standing frames on an end table. Then she clutched the album against her chest. "All these gifts today. Linda too. She gave me a clock radio and set all the stations for me, so I can listen to them at night when I can't sleep. And a new TV as well! I have good friends," she said, sounding astonished and overjoyed.

"That is because you are a good friend," I said, hustling off to the kitchen before I turned into a big blubbering mess in front of Mrs. Tomblin.

"Hey Phoebe," Collin was standing right behind me, "it's pleasant here, huh?" he whispered. "Mrs. Tomblin, she'll be looked after. There is staff on call, she'll make new friends, and when I called Constable Patchett an hour ago she told me what she told you – the police are confident they will be able to recover the other photographs. Mrs. Tomblin will have kept her promise to her aunt, after all."

I nodded, sniffling, feeling really emotional.

"I know, I know," Colin said softly.

I knew what he meant. Mrs. Tomblin had the right attitude – you were happy for what was, as she was right now. And what wasn't to be, well, there wasn't much you could do about that except be unhappy and that didn't change anything, anyhow.

chapter twenty-four

I was packing my clothes and gear for my visit to Grandy's. I was leaving tomorrow by bus. Both Greg and Matt had offered to drive me if I had been willing to wait until the weekend, which I wasn't. I was too eager to see Grandy.

I loved being with her, but most of all, I kept remembering what Aunt Debbie had said about Grandy's loneliness. Her circumstances weren't anything like those of Mrs. Tomblin, but all the same, she was lonely.

There was a knock on my door. Only Greg knocked.

"Left anything behind?" he joked as he gestured at the giant suitcase spread open on my bed. I'd borrowed one of Mom's, the largest one she had. I didn't need to take much, since I was only going for two weeks. Yet I couldn't stop myself from packing way more than was necessary. I guess Mom's super-planning genes were finally starting to bloom.

I shrugged. "I have a boatload of gifts for Grandy, Aunt

Debbie, Chris, Adam, and friends at school. Plus, I like to be prepared."

I glanced down at my watch. Our dinner reservation was an hour off. Since Greg was a stickler for routine, the fact that he'd scheduled a dinner on Wednesday evening, and hadn't invited Jonathan and Michelle – bonus! – only shored up my certainty about what we were going to be celebrating at this family dinner.

Lately my mom had been very tired all the time. At first I'd supposed it was from juggling the care of Elspeth and the volunteer work she was doing for the food bank. When she wasn't calling food distributors to donate supplies, she was working at her laptop on spreadsheets, doing budget projections. However, it was all those trips to the bathroom that were the key clue. Mom was in and out of there more than any room in the house – as she'd been in the early months of her pregnancy with Elspeth.

Jonathan's presence would have killed the celebration. Of course, it would have been satisfying to see him choke on his high-priced dinner (since Greg always paid, Jonathan and Michelle always ordered the most expensive items on the menu), but that moment would be coming soon enough for Jonathan. Greg was having lunch with him next week.

I was thrilled for my mom and Greg and to be a big sister to another sister or brother (a miniature Matt, please!). The only drawback was the prospect of another round of studio portraits after the birth of the baby.

Still, the next set of family pictures might not be a gruesome replay. I'd shown my mom the catalogue that Colin had lent me from Rachel Malick's exhibition. She thought the photos were fantastic and asked if she could show the catalogue to Greg. So maybe there was hope that after the next Creighton arrived on the scene, our family photos might be more Malick-style than waxwork museum.

"Your mother and I need to talk to you," Greg said, looking uneasy. All this was out of the ordinary for Greg, whose philosophy was to be Mr. Cool while those around him got frazzled.

Like me right now. Was there some problem already with the pregnancy? I followed Greg down the stairs to the living room where Mom was sitting on the sofa. Greg sat down on one side of her. She reached out and took my hand, and I sat down on the other side. She didn't let go of my hand, making it as clammy as hers was.

"Is there something wrong with your pregnancy?" I asked nervously. What else it could be? My mom was clearly worried about something.

"You guessed?" she asked. "How?"

"Moooom!" The way I stretched her name made her smile and Greg too. "When you're not glued to Elspeth or your laptop, you've been living in the bathroom. Hello! I was around, after all, when you were pregnant with Elspeth. Congratulations, that's terrific!" I kissed Mom, then stood up, leaned over her, and gave Greg a quick peck on the cheek, pleasantly startling him.

"No, no, it's not your mother's pregnancy. She's fine," he said.

"Except for the nausea, vomiting, head-spinning, exhaustion," Mom said, rolling her eyes. "That will pass."

Her pregnancy was fine. So, why were she and Greg still shooting anxious glances at each other?

"Grandy is in the hospital," Mom said. "She was standing

on a lawn chair on the porch, drilling in hooks for planters. She lost her balance and tumbled over."

"Is she badly hurt?"

"Your grandmother broke her left arm and fractured her hip. It will take months to heal because of her age – the hip especially. She'll need surgery and months of rehab," Greg said.

Grandy was accustomed to being really active and taking care of everybody else. Who was going to take care of Grandy once she left the hospital, if it took months for her to heal? "Can I speak to her now? What's the number at the hospital?"

"Phoebe, she's been sedated. You can speak to her tomorrow," Mom said.

"We're going right away to see Grandy, aren't we?" I asked, looking first at Mom, then at Greg.

Mom let go of my hand and wrapped an arm around my shoulder. "We are going to drive up on Saturday."

"Why the wait?" I asked, realizing I sounded ticked off with them for not leaving immediately.

"We all want to be with Grandy right now," Mom said quickly.

"Your grandmother will be heavily sedated to control the pain she is experiencing. I would like to examine her myself," Greg said. "I have a bypass surgery scheduled tomorrow, but then I am going to take a few days off so I can oversee her care – meet with her doctors. I've asked my friend Juan Fernandez, a top orthopedic surgeon, to meet us at the hospital on Saturday afternoon. I want him to go over Grandy's X-rays and scans, and consult with her doctors."

"You, Elspeth, and I will stay after Greg goes back on

Tuesday," Mom said, concerned that I'd think she was shuffling Grandy off as I had accused her of doing earlier this summer. "Aunt Debbie, Chris, and Adam are watching over her for now. We'll be with her soon too."

I guess Mrs. Tomblin's situation was on both of our minds. This wasn't the same, I told myself. My mom cared. So did Greg. And I needed to thank him, pronto. This was one of those instances – and there were probably more of them than I would admit to – where I was very grateful for Greg's take-charge perfectionism. I knew he would make sure Grandy was getting the best treatment and care.

"Thanks Greg." We hugged awkwardly, more like a scrimmage huddle than a hug...but that was a change, a nice one, for both of us.

"Please, no thanks are necessary. Grandy is family. If I am not satisfied with the level of her care, I'll make arrangements to have her brought to Toronto for treatment. Whatever should be done for Grandy, will be done," Greg said decisively. He looked down at his watch. "Matt will be waiting for us at the restaurant. Are you up to going?"

I nodded, as did my mom.

"Then we'd better leave," Greg said. "Don't want to keep Matt waiting and wondering. I called him on his cell and left him a message that we'd be a little late."

Someone else – like Jonathan – would have made a snarky remark about Matt getting a taste of his own medicine because Matt usually kept *us* waiting. Not Greg, though. This was another example of the up side of Greg's high standards, making it easier to look beyond his faults to the decent person he truly was.

chapter twenty-five

I recognized every nurse in the nursing station closest to Grandy's hospital room. And they recognized all of us too; our family practically camped out there. In shifts, though. There wasn't enough space for all of us at one time in the tiny private room Greg had insisted on for the duration of Grandy's hospitalization. The communal ward she'd been in had housed seven other patients.

Greg had left, satisfied with the care Grandy was receiving from the doctors in Barrie. The fact that Dr. Fernandez had backed up their diagnosis, course of treatment, and rehabilitation schedule soothed any of Greg's lingering doubts that a small hospital in Barrie could provide a level of care equal to a major hospital like his.

Greg had told us we should be very grateful indeed that Grandy had an uncomplicated hip fracture. If the surgery went well, and there were no post-op complications, she should be able to walk around in a few days. He'd offered to make the arrangements to have her moved to Toronto to the orthopedic hospital, and then to have her stay in a swanky private rehabilitation center in Toronto.

Grandy had been very touched by his offer and everything he'd done for her. Still, she wanted to stay in Barrie and recover in her own home – even after Greg had told her (scared the dickens out of her and us) what she had to watch out for while recovering. Infections, blood clots, pneumonia, falling again and fracturing the fracture topped the list.

I'd spoken to Aunt Debbie last night. She'd asked Grandy to live with them until she was fully recovered. Aunt Debbie's house had two bedrooms, and only one bathroom upstairs. Since Grandy wasn't going to be able to handle stairs for a while that meant she'd be stuck upstairs most of the time.

Instead, Chris was going to stay with Grandy until she was able to be on her own again – that could take up to three months, her doctor said. This was fantastic for Grandy, but was going to be tough on Chris, who was in her last year of high school and needed to get top grades to qualify for scholarship money for university.

The solution, as I saw it, was for me to move back to Grandy's for the fall semester and assist Chris so she would have the time to concentrate on her studies. Plus, I wanted to be part of the team of taking care of Grandy. She had always been there for me. It was my turn now to be there for her.

I had a long talk about this with Mom and Greg. At the start Greg had been against it, ticking off one by one his "reasonable objections"– the effect it would have on my schooling; that it would be hard for my mom in the first trimester of her pregnancy to handle Elspeth on her own; and last but not least (yet another in the series of nice surprises from Greg), I would be really missed.

My mom, though, had stood up for me, and stood up to Greg – a bit hesitantly at first. *Way to go Mom!* I felt like shouting that, but it would have ruined the spirit of the moment. She said that Grandy needed to be in her home and would adore having me and Chris with her. She would make arrangements for my teachers at Dunvegan to supervise my studies at my old school in Barrie for the fall semester.

I hadn't been able to sleep, I was that excited about sharing the news with Grandy. She'd had a bad night with a lot of pain and hadn't been able to rest comfortably. She was finally asleep now, according to Gretchen, the head nurse, when I called early this morning.

Even though I was already on the second round of my Tour de Forest Hill, I was pedaling as ferociously as when I began, pumped with nervous energy.

My first pit stop had been at Mrs. Tomblin's. She'd been playing gin rummy with three other ladies in the club room. That was an encouraging sight. I'd hung around for a half hour, then got all restless again and took off, pedaling over to Max's Marketplace. I'd hung out with Colin there during his break, filling him in about Grandy.

I couldn't wait a second longer to see if Grandy was awake and could talk on the phone. I braked, went onto the sidewalk, and took out my BlackBerry. Please, please let Grandy answer,

I prayed as I punched in the extension to her room.

"Hello," Grandy answered, sounding groggy and unsure. Usually her hello boomed so loudly out of the phone receiver it blasted right into your eardrum.

"Grandy, it's me! Phoebe."

I heard the rumble of her laugh.

"I'm not that drugged up. I can still make out the voices of my relatives," she said. "When I can't, please put me out in my boat and set me sailing on Lake Simcoe."

I would have laughed, or at least smiled at that old joke Grandy always made, but I couldn't, not after meeting Mrs. Tomblin and seeing what it was like for her to be forgetting parts of her life, one piece at a time. "How are you feeling, Grandy?"

"Been better," she barked out. "What's in these drugs they're giving me? I sound like your Grandfather Clark, may he rest in peace."

I took a deep breath and rushed out my spiel about wanting to move back in with her along with Chris, and then why it would be best for her...and for me too. The final argument was that my mom and Greg thought it was a great idea too.

There was silence. Well, not really silence, there was the wheezy breathing of Grandy and my light panting to catch my breath. "Sweetie, I've been hoping you would come back. Every time I pass your room I keep wishing you were there, next to me," Grandy said, now sounding like she was struggling not to cry.

"I'll be there soon, knocking on your wall," I said.

"Can't wait!"

And neither could I.

chapter twenty-six

"Got room in that trunk of yours for the Paul Norman so-called thrillers for your family? Matt kidded, eyeing my huge suitcase.

"Of course," I said.

"In fact, that suitcase looks big enough to hold Paul Norman himself – even without having to dismember him first, although everyone who has had the privilege of assisting him in the editorial process wouldn't mind, *moi* included. Alas, I will have to satisfy my homicidal fantasies with merely dismembering his prose," Matt said.

He had made sure Paul Norman had autographed copies of his latest novel for Grandy and Aunt Debbie, who were devoted fans. As he was stretching his hand across the small tabletop to hand me the books, Matt sent his chocolate donut flying straight across to the next table. Mine was already safely stored in my stomach.

"See, even his books are a menace. Curses!" he hissed dramatically.

I giggled. Matt had insisted on meeting up with me at a donut shop near the bus terminal. He had also insisted on driving me to Barrie when Greg had been called in early this morning to do emergency bypass surgery.

I had insisted he and his friend go ahead with their plans to see productions of *Richard III* in the afternoon and *Othello* in the evening (a double dose of Shakespeare that would have finished me off just like it did most of the characters in those tragedies).

The donut shop meeting was our compromise. I was going to miss Matt like anything. In fact, there were more people beyond my family that I was going to miss like anything, more than I would have imagined a few months back.

Like Mrs. Tomblin whom I'd gone to see yesterday to say good-bye. She'd become as emotional as I'd ever seen her, embracing me and making me promise to write and call often. I would. I'd invited her to come up for Thanksgiving for the big family shindig Aunt Debbie was already organizing. Greg was going to drive everybody there in his SUV, though Matt teased if everyone packed like I did, maybe Greg needed to consider renting a U-Haul.

I reached over and took Matt's hand. "Can't wait to see you in Barrie. You better show up. No excuses," I said.

"I never thought I'd say this, but Barrie, here I come," he said.

"You're such a city slicker!" A park was about as much of the outdoors as Matt could stomach.

"You're such a nature girl!" That was true. Soon I would

be biking, not on city streets, but bike trails, and doing all the nature-girl stuff I loved to do: hike, camp out, fish.

Matt gave me one last big hug, then left. I ordered another donut and a chocolate milk as I waited for Colin and Yuri, who had arrived last night from Tokyo. Boy, would I miss them like anything too.

A trip to Barrie would be a short jaunt for the globe-trotting Tokyo Miss Marple, Yuri had reassured me when I'd texted her. And Colin loved the outdoors as much as I did. He'd never been to Barrie and the bus ride didn't cost much, so he intended to visit, too, and go fishing and hiking with me.

"Hi and bye!" Yuri swept down on me, embracing me so tightly my nose was flattened against her T-shirt.

"Hey, I need that nose!" I groused.

"I come, you go. Not fair!" she said, flopping onto the chair Matt had just vacated.

"What's with you? You've gone all hip on me!" I said.

She had new cat's eye red-framed glasses. She'd grown out her hair. It was razor cut in various lengths to above her shoulders, and she was wearing an eyelet cami over skinny Capri jeans.

"Might as well as vamp it up while I can. Soon it's back to scratchy gray wool kilts, white shirts, knee socks, and oxfords," she said. "You won't get the chance to miss me, you goof, because I'm going to be a regular little commuter to Barrie."

"What's a mere hour-long bus trip to Barrie to a world traveler like you?" I teased, thrilled to hear that.

"What's the scoop on you and Colin?"

Colin. Even with Yuri, I couldn't say how strongly I felt about Colin and how much I would miss him. I was embarrassed about how much. I hoped the Tokyo Miss Marple wouldn't figure that out, but I couldn't count on it.

"The Marple sisters, together at last!"

Yuri and I didn't have to look up to know who had said that.

There was Colin coming toward us, backpack hanging loosely off his right shoulder and a large gift bag in his hand.

"Thanks! We're better-looking, better-dressed and decades younger than she is. Smarter, no. No one is smarter than Miss Marple!" Yuri shot back. "I could call you Hercule Poirot, how you'd like that?" she teased.

He grimaced. "I would tell you you're full of hot air. My head's not the shape of an egg. I'm way over five and half feet. I don't have a waxed moustache—"

"But your little gray cells are as sharp. No sharper!" I said, looking straight at him and hoping my expression wasn't as lovey-dovey as I was feeling.

"Thank you for that, Miss," he said, standing next to me for a second before he went off to bring over another chair. His face was suspiciously red, as though he was feeling how I was feeling right now. Unfortunately, my little gray cells (as Hercule Poirot referred to his super computer of a brain) weren't in the league of Poirot, Yuri, or Colin. So what if I wasn't a brainy type – neither were lots of other people.

"You do your best, that's all you can do, and you don't beat yourself up about what you were not meant to do best!" Grandy had always said that to me as encouragement whenever I got frustrated with things I wasn't good at, like tennis or French.

Grandy. She'd had the surgery. It had gone well, but that didn't block out the list of possible post-op complications cited by Greg from replaying in his head. I recited a silent prayer for Grandy's full recovery.

"Hey, you're going all gloomy on us, and the bus hasn't even left the terminal!" Yuri said, pinching my cheek.

"Ow, that hurts!"

"Natural blush," she said, then whispered, "Like you or Colin need blush. Jeez, you both have tomato faces!"

"Yeah, yeah, like you didn't every time you saw Anthony!" I said. Yuri had dated Anthony for a while until she realized what a super-sexist jerk he was.

"Don't remind me!" she groaned. "What was I thinking? I wasn't thinking. Save me from my bad taste, okay?"

"I tried, you wouldn't listen!"

Yuri gave a big sigh. "Yeah, I wouldn't. Now I won't have you around to do that anymore."

"Only for the fall semester."

"I'm holding you to that!" Then glancing at Colin, she whispered, "At least one of us has good taste."

I got nervous suddenly, wondering how Colin would treat me in front of Yuri. Like a friend? Like a girlfriend?

When he returned with a chair, he placed his backpack on the ground and as he handed me the gift bag, he bent close... and kissed me. In front of Yuri! Definitely girlfriend!

A second later, Yuri kicked my ankle. I kicked her back.

I was ecstatic, then I felt sad, missing Colin and Yuri already, and I wasn't even gone yet.

"For me?" I teased.

"Who else?" he said, sitting down next to me. "Yuri in person and not on a BlackBerry! Man, you text fast... and cogitate even faster. You should seriously consider something in the crime field."

"That would freak my parents out," Yuri said, laughing, but flattered all the same. I could tell by the wide smile on her face. "The Tokyo Miss Marple will take your suggestion under consideration. And here's some more detecting for you. To my detecting eye, that looks like a photo album in the gift bag."

Not only could Yuri's fingers text at supersonic speed, they could snatch even faster. Before I could even bend over to look into the gift bag to see if Yuri had detected correctly, she had the album out and on the table.

"I got the idea from the album you made for Mrs. Tomblin," Colin said. His flush, which had almost faded away, flared tomato red again. "So you wouldn't forget!"

I leafed through the pages quickly, but would go over them slowly on the bus and every day in Barrie until I returned home to Toronto – pleased by the sudden revelation that I considered Toronto home now.

Skimming through, I felt the whole mix of emotions that Mrs. Tomblin had felt when she leafed through her album. Glad to remember, but teary all the same.

There were the pictures taken at the last garage sale of Mrs. Tomblin and me in the garage and Colin and Mrs. Tomblin in the living room. Pictures of my mom handing Elspeth to me to hold the day Colin had come over to check out the negatives I was keeping for Mrs. Tomblin. Shots of Matt, Mrs. Tomblin, and me on Matt's balcony the afternoon Colin had popped by to see how she was doing. And a whole bunch of snapshots of Colin taken by me.

"Something essential is missing," Yuri said. She was standing behind me so she could look through the album. "Or should I say some*one*. Hint, hint."

There were no photos of Yuri, and as I turned around to look at her, Colin whipped his camera out of his backpack and started snapping shots of me and Yuri. Then he got a lady waiting for a bus to Niagara Falls to take photos of all three of us.

The loudspeaker was announcing that my bus was ready for boarding. I started to close the album and noticed that half of the pages were empty. As I turned to ask Colin about that, he said, "I kept those blank for all the new photos of when I," he cleared his throat, "I mean we, visit you and your grandmother in Barrie."

"I promise to take up a lot of that space," Yuri said, wrapping her arm through mine.

"Me too!" Colin said shyly, reddening as I wrapped my arm through his and we stood there together.

I was going to have many new photos to add to my collection of old photographs. Those too, would become old photographs, a treasure chest of an album filled with people I cared for and my good memories of them.

I wouldn't need a photograph to remember this moment, though, this very happy moment, standing arm in arm with Yuri and Colin. I'd remember it as long as I could remember.

about the author

Sherie Posesorski is a Toronto freelance writer and editor whose work has appeared in *The New York Times*, *The Globe and Mail*, *The Vancouver Sun*, and the *Toronto Star*, among others. She is the author of *Escape Plans*, a children's novel, and *Shadow Boxing*, a novel for young adults.